Between the ages of 22-64, Alan enjoyed a career in model-making and owned his own model-making company from 1985 to 2010, designing and producing models for architects, film and TV, exhibitions and museums. In 2005, he completed a creative writing course, and it was at this time that he wrote this story for his two elder daughters, Holly and Poppy. Alan is now 76 years old and lives in Hertfordshire, with his four children, where he enjoys reading and collecting antiques.

For my four children: Holly, Poppy, George and Daisy.

A. E. Mount

POLLY, ANNA AND THE BARN PATROL

AUSTIN MACAULEY PUBLISHERS™

LONDON • CAMBRIDGE • NEW YORK • SHARJAH

A CIP catalogue record for this title is available from the British Library.

ISBN 9781398419247 (Paperback)
ISBN 9781398419254 (ePub e-book)

www.austinmacauley.com

First Published 2022
Austin Macauley Publishers Ltd®
1 Canada Square
Canary Wharf
London
E14 5AA

Thanks to Austin Macauley Publishers.

Chapter 1
An Amazing Discovery

I still get that tingling feeling up my spine whenever I think back to the day we discovered the old typewriter in the garden shed.

It happened by accident. We were looking for a little fishing net which I remembered seeing in the shed the last time we were in there; it was blue, and blue is my favourite colour.

Polly, my kitten sister, had discovered that the frog spawn down in the spinney-pond was turning into tadpoles and she had this idea, to bring some home as a surprise for Poppy and Holly.

The moment we peered round the shed door; I spotted the blue net sticking out of the top shelf.

"It's up on the top shelf," I said, but she was off before I had finished the sentence.

She'd scrambled up the shed wall, crawled along the shelf and grabbed the net in her teeth. She tugged at it, but the net must have caught on a nail or something. Pulling hard backwards, she stepped straight off the shelf, where she hung, wriggling, for a split second, before falling, with an almighty crash, in a cloud of dust, onto a heap of junk piled on the bench beneath.

The net sprang off the nail and disappeared down behind her, hitting something which made a funny click sound followed by a DING!

I rushed over to see if Polly was alright.

"It was the only way to get it," she said gruffly, from her cloud of dust and proceeded to shake and brush herself off.

I was more interested in what had made the click-DING! sound, and, pushing the rubbish and a grumpy Polly aside, I soon found it.

Sitting on the back of the worktop was a big black metal thing covered with round discs, on each of these discs were written, both numbers and the letters of the alphabet muddled up in a strange order, and behind everything was the top of a sheet of paper with the letter 'P' on it stamped in fine bold print. On the bottom of the machine was an important looking sign saying…

"The American Typewriter Co. Inc. Delaware."

I found the 'O' tab and hit it for fun, to my surprise and joy…click DING! an O arrived next to the P. I quickly followed with L-L-Y and there on the paper was written—POLLY—as bold as you like.

"Polly!" I shouted, "come and look at this."

She came scurrying over.

"I found this yellow bucket, there were some other coloured ones, but I thought that this would go nicely with the blue net."

"Forget that for a minute," I replied. "I think I've made a big discovery…we CAN write."

"We can't, stupid, we've tried, and we can't."

"Well, just come and take a look at this," I said, and led her over to where the machine sat on the bench. I had removed the rubbish and cleaned it up a bit.

I quickly pressed the discs A-N-N-A, and after all the clicks and dings, there on the paper was written POLLYANNA.

"I've missed out the 'and', but there, what do you think?"

She read Pollyanna on the paper and gaped in surprise as I continued with—AND THE TADPOLE ADVENTURE.

"Don't you see," I said to her excitedly. "Now, I can write about all our adventures.

"Of course, we'll have to keep this a big secret. We'll hide the machine in the corner on the bench behind some cardboard boxes and it can be our office. Won't it be fun?"

"It sounds great but right now we've got an adventure to do. I've got the bucket; you get the net and let's go tadpoling."

Chapter 2
The Tadpole Adventure

So, off we went, that afternoon, to the pond. We threw some titbits into the bucket for a little picnic, and, as the lawn had been mown that morning, I put a small bag of grass in for the lambs.

On the way across the back-field, Polly tried to creep up on anything she could see, butterflies and dragonflies mostly, but when she tried to stalk a magpie, it began to play a game of tease with her and so she gave up.

We were passing a tall clump of nettles, when out jumped a lamb. Polly was more surprised than I, and she dropped the bucket.

"Look what you made me do," she said, angrily to the lamb.

"Never mind, let me help you pick up your bits and pieces."

"It's quite alright," said Polly, indignantly, "We can manage ourselves, thank you very much."

"Don't be so silly, Polly," I said. "There's no need to get all uppish just because somebody plays a trick on you for a change."

Polly didn't say much after that, and, after helping us pick the things up, the little lamb ambled along beside us.

"What are you up to?"

"Nothing!" said Polly sharply.

She was still a little upset, so I said, "Come on Polly, cheer up, it's about time we made a few friends."

So, Polly and Lindy, that was the lamb's name, made friends and we told her about our plan to take some tadpoles home for Holly and Poppy.

"Won't they wonder who did it?" she said.

"Oh, we'll leave them round by the front door," I said. "They'll think that one of the neighbours left them."

"What about the bucket?" asked Lindy. "Surely they'll recognise it."

"Oh, Lindy!" snapped Polly impatiently. "Questions! Questions! Questions! The children are always leaving their toys laying about out the front, so shut up and let's get on. We've brought you some fresh grass so that you can picnic with us by the pond…it's a lovely day, don't you think?"

I knew then that Polly and Lindy would be the best of friends.

The three of us soon reached the trees which shaded the edge of the pond and decided to eat our picnic right away. We sat munching and watching the frogspawn bubbling away. A bright blue dragonfly caught my attention as it whizzed from one lily pad to another, and I dozed off for a minute.

But not for long.

"Anna!" shouted Polly, "Are you fishing or sleeping?"

"Fishing," I replied, and scampered down the bank to join them.

"We've got a plan," said Lindy.

"Let's hear it," I replied. "But if it means me getting wet, forget it."

"No, you'll be alright," said Polly. "See that log floating near the bank? Well, Lindy's been out on it and didn't fall off, so we thought that if we put the pole of the net through the bucket handle, the same way we plan to carry it home."

"Yes," I said.

"And then Lindy takes one end onto the log."

"Yes," I said.

"I'll be on the bank with the other end, and we can scoop the tadpoles up in the bucket."

"Oh, and you see that branch laying on the bank? We want you to keep the log steady with that; 'that's if it starts wobbling."

"I thought you said it was safe?" I queried.

"Well, it did wobble a little bit and Lindy managed to jump off, but I'm sure that with your expert assistance, everything will be alright," went on Polly, with a grin.

"Sounds a bit dodgy to me," I said.

"Oh, come on Anna, be a sport," shouted Lindy, already balancing on the log.

"Okay," I said. "But the plan doesn't sound fool-proof to me. Anything could happen."

And everything did.

They passed the pole through the handle of the bucket and Lindy edged out on the log, whilst I steadied it with the branch.

Polly was on the bank with the other end, and the two of them lowered it beneath the pond's surface by leaning forward and dipping their paws right under the water. As Lindy leant forward, the log moved further away from the bank, and I struggled hard to pull it back with the branch.

Polly and Lindy stood up bringing a bucket full of tadpoles. The log began wobbling and they couldn't stop it. Lindy let go of her end and Polly whipped it to the safety of the bank, losing a few tadpoles on the way, but poor old Lindy was left tottering on the wobbling log.

There was nothing we could do as she lost control and fell backwards over the other side of the log.

I heard Polly give a little giggle and couldn't stop a smile myself, as the lamb bobbed up to the surface with water weed hanging from her head like a green wig.

"Did you save the tadpoles?" she shouted out, sportingly.

"Yes," laughed Polly. "Are you OKAY?"

"Yes, fine. Lucky I learnt to swim in the sheep-dip last week. What happened to you, Anna?"

"I'm afraid I couldn't hold it," I replied.

"Don't sound so sheepish, Anna," shouted Polly, with a laugh.

"Get it! Sheepish," and started to dance around whooping with laughter until she collapsed on the bank.

Meanwhile, a soggy lamb emerged from the pond and proceeded to roll around on the grass wiping the mud and stuff off.

"Well, we've certainly got a bucket full of tadpoles," said Lindy, sitting down, rather damp, on the side of the pond. "I hope Holly and Poppy appreciate them."

"Oh, I'm sure they will. They've been talking about getting some for a week now, but Mum and Dad won't let them come down to the pond on their own."

"Jolly good," she said. "So come on, I'll dry off helping you back home with our catch. It's been great fun playing with you both. I hope we can have some more fun soon."

So, the three of us walked back in the warmth of the afternoon sun. Lindy soon dried off and, on the way, she told us about the different creatures that lived in the field and hedgerows that encircled the back-field. "Most of them are friendly, but Mum says that, sometimes at night, there's an old fox that stalks around. I don't like the sound of him, and I can't say that I trust the magpies and crows much either. The other birds have a right old time chasing the magpies out of the hedgerows when they've got babies in their nests."

"Magpies!" said Polly. "I chased one off only this morning," she continued, giving me a quick look. Hmmm I thought, I rather think that it nearly chased you off Polly, but I didn't say anything to upset her. As you've probably noticed, she gets a bit touchy.

We finally arrived at the hole in the fence, and having helped us through with the bucket, Lindy said goodbye and we all promised to meet up the next day.

Polly and I crept round the front and put the bucket next to the milk bottles on the front step, returned the net to the shed and went in to see what was for tea.

Chapter 3
The Pirate Ship

Later on, as I was slowly tapping out our day's adventure, it occurred to me that there was only one sheet of paper to write on. Polly and I searched the shed from top to bottom, but we couldn't find any more. The answer came to me later whilst I was dozing on the back of Dad's chair. In the top room of the house is an old roll-top desk where dad keeps all sorts of bits and pieces, and in that desk is a drawer full of sheets of paper, just the right size. I spotted them one day when dad was writing a letter. The problem is, how to get the paper to the back shed without the rest of the family seeing us? I suddenly came up with a great plan which turned out to be an adventure in itself.

The next day was as warm as ever and Polly and I decided to pop over the back fence to look for our new friend, Lindy lamb. We finally found her over at the pond. She had spent most of the morning trying to master the log pirate ship, and there she was, out in the middle of the pond, sitting astride the log, enjoying the sun.

She was very muddy of course, and she had a sword tied round her middle, a strange hat perched on top of her head and looked very much the pirate.

"Ahoy there cap'n," I shouted, "you puttin' to sea?"

"No," replied the lamb, "just practicing; come aboard."

"You won't catch me on that thing," shouted Polly, "you look a right mess, anyway. How could we come aboard? Even if we wanted to, you're right out in the middle."

"Well, you see that post further along the bank? Go and untie the string and you can pull me in."

What a clever lamb, I thought, as I followed after Polly, who had run down the bank, untied the string and was pulling the log in at a fair speed. Lindy was hanging on tight and Polly was doing her best to topple her into the water. However, she was unsuccessful. The log thumped into the bank and Lindy leapt off with great style, and upon landing, she swept off her hat and gave us a graceful bow.

"Lieutenant Lindy at your service. I'm afraid that the captains ashore but you're welcome to come aboard. I'll take you once round the lily pads for a handful of that delicious grass you had yesterday."

"We didn't bring any today," I replied. "There's a pile back in the garden. You can have some later, but tell us, where did you find the hat, the string and the sword?"

"The sword, I made myself," she said proudly, and with lightning speed, she pulled it out and had Polly pinned against the nearest tree, the sword pointed at her tummy. "The hat and the string I found in the barn over by the house, the feather I got from a magpie". Now, young kitten, you were trying to board my log without my permission. I've a mind to make ye walk the plank."

"Cut the silly sailor's talk, Lindy," said Polly, looking a little outsmarted. "I wasn't trying to get on your silly old log, I can't swim anyway."

"You can't swim?" said the lamb with a laugh and, dropping the sword, pushed Polly into the pond with a splash!

It wasn't deep enough to be dangerous, and I'm sure Lindy knew this. She just wanted to get one over on Polly, who, she thought, was a bit too cocky for her liking. I found it hard not to laugh. Polly, on the other hand soon learnt to swim a bit and finally clambered out onto the log, a large lump of weed draped over one eye, and we all laughed ourselves silly.

"Looks like you've got a new crew member," I said, as we both pushed the log out, it sailed out to the end of its string and bobbed gently amongst the lilies, a very proud Polly laying on her back whilst two bright blue dragonflies played kiss-chase over her head.

I had been thinking for some time, that we had not only found ourselves a very jolly little friend in Lindy, but that she was pretty clever too. It hadn't taken her long to get this pirate adventure together, including, mastering the log, finding the string and hat, working out the clever mooring post and making a sword as well.

She was now laying down watching as the dragonflies buzzed around her new chum, lazing out on the log.

"Lindy?" I said, after a few minutes, "is there any more string where that came from?"

"Lots," replied the Lamb.

Later, we walked back through the tall grass towards the old barn. Lindy and Polly were now good friends, the pirate adventure seemed to have bonded them together and they certainly made a grand crew playing on the log right through the morning and half the afternoon. It was now getting late, and the sun was sinking low and orange over the pond behind us as we followed our shadows towards home.

"The barn is very handy as a shelter for us when it rains," said Lindy, "the mummy sheep also have their babies in there too and later on in the summer when it gets really hot we all come here for a haircut, I haven't had my hair cut yet but my mum says that it's the most beautiful feeling in the whole world, like taking all your clothes off on a hot day.

"You mean to say you were born in that old barn," said Polly, and then paused in thought. "What is it, Polly?" I asked. "You know," she said, "I just had a funny thought, a distant memory of when you and I were small, Anna, there was a barn very much like our own."

"You're probably remembering the farm in Kent where we were born," I replied. "Memory is a funny thing like that. It takes something to trigger it off, if you close your eyes tightly, you might even see Mum and Dad."

Polly stopped still and squeezed her eyes shut for a long time and I've never before seen such a lovely smile as the one that spread over my dear Polly's face.

"Come on, you two!" cried Lindy, who had reached the large entrance to the barn. "Now, don't mind if you see things scurrying around up the dark end; they're the barn rats. I've made friends with two of them, their names are Robert and Royston. I think that's a bit posh, so I call them Rob and Roy. They are twins, their mum and dad and the rest of their family aren't so friendly though. They have been known to get pretty fierce if anyone digs around at the dark end, but Rob and Roy are friendly. In fact, they gnawed off the lengths of string for me this morning, I wonder if they are around now? By the way, Anna what did you want the string for?"

"Ah!" I said. "I will show you later. After seeing how quickly you sorted out your pirate ship, this morning I might need your help with my design."

"What design?" asked Polly, all ears. "You're not making a pirate ship too. I bet it won't be as good as Lindy's. No, silly," I said. "This is much more difficult than a pirate ship!"

Chapter 4
The Fairy Run Thing

So, the three of us sat on the warm straw in the barn doorway and I told them my plan.

"It's like this," I began. "You know that we've only got one piece of paper in our magic word machine, Polly—and it's not enough if we want to write down all our adventures; well, I know where there's lots more."

"Where?" interrupted Polly, and Lindy sat with her mouth open, speechless. I was just beginning to tell them about the roll…top desk and the drawer full of paper, when Lindy said.

"Wait a minute you two, do you mean to tell me that you can write? And that you're writing about your adventures—I don't believe it, you can't! Only people can write!"

So, we told Lindy about our discovery in the shed, of our little cardboard office and that she was already starring in our first story.

Lindy was as pleased as punch and even more pleased to think that we wanted her to join us in our bigger adventure. When the excitement had cooled down, I told them my plan.

"The string is a very important part of my design, and you discovering this whole bundle of string in the barn, is the most important thing that has happened today."

"What's more important than Lindy's pirate ship and more important than me seeing Mum and Dad in my memory in the field?" piped in Polly.

"Nothing can be more important than the memory of our Mum and Dad," I replied, "but it is important in our new adventure. You see I've been digging around a bit more in the shed and I've found some old books about people called 'Boy Scouts', it's got drawings of how to tie string together with things called knots; very much like the one you tied your log up with Lindy. In fact, Lindy, I think you'd make a pretty good Boy Scout."

"She can't, she's a girl," butted in Polly.

"Oh, never mind," I said. "Well, on the next page was a picture of a thing called an aerial runway."

All the time I had been telling the other two about my discoveries, I began to see, first one and then two sets of little yellow slit eyes appear in the gathering gloom at the far end of the barn. Then, another pair and then another, until a whole line of little eyes appeared, all looking at us from the darkness. I told the others quietly. Lindy stayed still but Polly could not help herself and quickly turned round to look. All the eyes went out, except for four. Lindy slowly turned around and whispered, "Hey Rob…Roy, it's me. Come and meet my two new friends."

"We don't like cats!"

"We don't like cats!" said two voices, both together, from the darkness.

"These two are different," said Lindy, "and I think they may need your help."

"WE DON'T LIKE CATS!"

"WE DON'T LIKE CATS!" sang out the two voices again.

"Well, you know that string you cut me into lengths this morning, we want some more."

"What! More pirate ships?"

"What! More pirate ships?" said the voices.

"No, this is something much bigger and much more important. It's for a fairy run-thing."

"An aerial runway!" I corrected, and the two voices replied:

"What's an aerial runway?"

"What's an aerial runway?" but by this time they had forgotten their shyness and crept right up to within a few feet of us.

"See," said Lindy. "I told you these cats were cool. Now come out here and listen to Anna's plan. We will most certainly need your help.

Rob and Roy came over and sat in the hay near to us and I said, "I know. I'll quickly nip over the fence to the shed and bring back the book."

When I returned, the other four were in serious conversation. Rob and Roy were saying that they'd heard that a new family of foxes had arrived in the next field and had dug a deep den there.

"We'll have to sort that out later," I said, and I opened the Boy Scout book at the page with the aerial runway picture on it.

"WOW!"

"WOW!" shouted Rob and Roy with glee. Polly and Lindy gaped in wonder.

"We can't make that," said Lindy.

"Oh yes, we can!"

"Oh yes, we can!" sang Rob and Roy.

"I'm game," said Polly.

There, in front of us was a wonderful picture of some Boy Scouts swooping down from a large tree towards the ground using a rope which was fixed to the top of the tree and sloping a long way to a post which was banged into the ground.

"Right, we'll get the string, you find the tree."

"Right, we'll get the string, you find the tree," said Rob and Roy.

"Hold on guys!!" I cried. "Slow down everyone, we're only using the aerial runway idea, to get the paper down from the bathroom window to the back shed, we don't need a tree."

"What paper? And what shed?"

"What paper? And what shed?" said the two rats.

I then began to explain our plan to Rob and Roy, who, just like Lindy, were very pleased to know that they were also staring in our adventure story, but they asked that the rest of their family wasn't to be mentioned as their dad wouldn't like it.

"They are a secret lot, see."

"They are a secret lot, see." Seemed to sum it up. The next day, we put our aerial runway plan to the test. It was a Sunday and luckily Mum, Dad and the children had driven off on a trip to see some relatives. Rob and Roy arrived with the coil of string. Polly and I took it upstairs, tied one end to the window catch in the bathroom and dropped the rest out of the window, down to the garden. Lindy arrived just in time to help Rob and Roy down to the bottom of the garden and tie it off to the knob on the shed door. Meanwhile, I scampered up to the top room to get the paper. When I returned, the other animals had checked that the string was long enough and were about to tie it to the shed doorknob.

"Wait a minute!" I cried, "I have to pass the string through the roll of paper first." I had rolled the sheets of paper up into a tube and secured it with a piece of Sellotape which I found in the top room.

"Okay!" shouted the team at the bottom of the garden, with excitement. "We'll tie off down here, you untie your end and pass it through the tube."

Polly sat on the window ledge, holding the tube of paper whilst I untied the string, threaded it through the tube and tied it back onto the window catch. But as I pulled the string tight, disaster happened.

Polly, who was waving and generally having fun with the others way down the end of the garden, felt the tube being tugged out of her grasp as I retied the string. She naturally clung on tighter, and as my knot pulled the string taut, off went the paper tube with Polly hanging off the bottom of it, just like the picture in the Boy Scout's book. I looked around and Polly was gone. All I heard was, "Weeeee! as Polly disappeared off down the string.

The three at the bottom of the garden didn't know what hit 'em, because Polly did exactly that; one minute they heard this 'Weeeee!' sound, and the next minute, they were a pile of tumbling animals as Polly crashed amongst them.

Lindy's fluffy woolly body helped cushion most of the blow and the four chums lay in a big heap, spluttering and laughing.

"WOW! That was really great," I heard Polly shout. "I'm going to have another go!"

"Is Polly okay?" I shouted from the window.

"Yes," came the chorus from the end of the garden and I saw Polly racing back up the garden towards the house.

"How's the tube of paper?" I shouted, and the other three turned round to see the tube resting safely against the doorknob at the end of the string.

"Fine!"

"Fine!"

"Fine!" all three shouted back in perfect harmony. So that was the story of the aerial runway, or the fairy run thing as Lindy still calls it. The rest of the day was spent playing on our new invention.

Polly, Rob and Roy spent hours running up to the bathroom then flying down the string using a little handle cleverly put together by Rob and Roy. In fact, the handle was so strong that the two little rats ended up sailing down together with a perfectly harmonic double...

Weeeee...

Weeeee...!

Myself, I was happy to get the roll of paper undone. I took Lindy into the cardboard office to show her the magic word machine and how it worked. She learnt how to use it pretty quickly and was soon banging away on the discs whilst I dictated the story that had just happened in the back garden.

Lindy and I had decided that we were too grown up and really too heavy to tackle the aerial runway, which turned out okay because by the time the sun was sinking, we had a very tired Polly, Rob and Roy, a new office clerk, appointed by me amongst lots of cheers and hurrahs. But most important of all, another chapter in our adventure book was laying safely on my cardboard desk in our cardboard office.

Chapter 5
Sam Stork

And so, the summer rolled on; sunny days and warm nights, the odd thunder shower of warm and welcome rain. When the family went away on a day trip, Polly, Rob and Roy would fetch out the aerial runway and play all day. Rob and Roy reported back regularly on the new family of foxes in the next field, but they kept to themselves, so everything drifted along quite peacefully. Lindy and I would often go down to the pond and lay in the grass talking about what things and animals there might be beyond our field.

We were laying there one day, when Lindy spotted something in the sky. It looked like some sort of a bird, but its movement was different than any other bird we'd seen before, and as it came nearer, because it was certainly coming our way, we could see that it flew with long slow flaps on enormous wings. I suddenly felt afraid and told Lindy to scramble into a near bramble thicket and I followed her, getting more than a few painful scratches on the way.

Just in time! The sky darkened with the shadow of the huge bird as it swooped low over us and landed silently into the water at the edge of the pond. It had the longest legs I'd ever seen and it's long, dangerous looking beak pointed down to the water as his keen eyes focused on some movement below the surface. We watched, quite rigid with fear. A flash of turquoise signalled the departure of the local kingfisher to the other end of the pond. Our new arrival was obviously fierce fishing competition. An observation which was immediately proved correct, as in the wink of an eye, the big grey bird had a fish wriggling in its beak. "Did you see that?" whispered Lindy.

"No, he was too quick," I replied.

But, unfortunately, with my last word, the bird's large head cocked around sideways in our direction. We both froze with fear. Up until now we had been watching this natural theatre unfolding in front of us; now we felt uncomfortably a part of it, and the hairs rose on the back of my neck as the bird silently took one foot and then the other from the water and slowly, walked towards our hiding place. The bird's silent approach was so frightening that I coughed in fright!

The spell was broken. "All right!" croaked the big bird, who had stopped and stood still and high above us, "You can come out. I only eat fish!"

And that's how we met Mr Croak the stork, for that's what we called him when he wasn't around.

We crawled out from under the bramble bush and washed our scratched noses in the pond, keeping one eye on the large stranger. "You'd have been better off if you had hidden in the long grass," said the bird. "I only land in the water."

He seemed quite chatty, so I asked, "Why haven't we seen you here before?"

"I only come down to this spinney each year towards the end of the summer. There's an especially tasty fish that lives here, and it gets to just the right size and flavour about this time of year."

Lindy and I gave each other a yucky look.

"I live away in that direction," and he swung his beak over in the direction beyond our barn. I've been down to where your spinney runs into the big river for a few days, and I thought that I'd drop in here for a little snack on my way home.

"How far's that?" asked Lindy her mouth agape in amazement. We both had wondered what was in the rest of the world and 'The Big River' sent thrills of excitement through us.

"How far is what?" replied the big bird. "My lake or the big river?"

"The Big River," we both said together.

"It's many, many miles," croaked the large bird, but it's only five hours on my big wings."

After a long talk about other places, the stork said his goodbyes, jumped into the air, and with two beats of his large grey wings climbed slowly into the sky; he rose up and over the barn. We watched him until he became a small dot in the sky, and finally the dot dropped away and disappeared behind the roof of the barn. Lindy and I ambled back across the field, chatting as we went about the world outside our field and what the stork had said about it. When we arrived back, the others were sitting at the barn doors and we both flopped on to the hay beside them.

"We saw a giant bird," said Rob, as soon as we arrived.

"It came from the direction of the pond and flew right over us," continued Polly. "You must have seen it."

"That's Mr Croak," said Lindy. "He's a stork and he gave Anna and me a nasty scare, but we soon made friends and he told us all about the big world outside. "Our Dad told us all about that," piped up Roy.

"Your dad hasn't been as far as Mr Croak," replied Lindy.

"No, but he's been as far as the wheelie bin in the industrial site up the road and he sometimes brings home a paper and it is all about the big world. They all worship something called Man U, and Dad says there are these sorts of clowns they call politicians. "Yes, but Mr Croak was telling us about forests and lakes, foxes and badgers, hills and valleys and where our stream joins the big river.

"How far is the big river?" asked Polly. I could see that she was getting excited about it all.

"Five hours on big wings," replied Lindy, standing as tall as she could with her arms crossed like the Indian Chief in Peter Pan.

"Cut the comedy you two. We've got a bit of a surprise for you. You should have noticed but you were all so full of your Mr Croak that you didn't. Polly said indignantly.

"What's that?" Lindy and I said, both together.

"Hey, that's it!" shouted Polly, clapping her paws together in delight. "Rob and Roy have lost it, and you and Lindy have caught it."

"What do you mean?" answered Lindy. "Do stop talking in riddles Polly."

"Well, today on the aerial runway, Rob and Roy were up in the bathroom window, all ready to jump, when something happened and Rob came sailing down all on his own, and when he reached the bottom Roy shouted, 'Are you all right?' And Rob shouted back, 'Yes, I'm fine,' and ever since then they've been able to speak separately."

"Yes," piped in Rob, on his own, "and then you two arrive back and start talking together like we used to." Everybody looked at each other and then burst into laughter and we all rolled around in the straw in a big happy bundle until we were all exhausted.

But we were all so very pleased for Rob and Roy.

After we had run out of laughter, Rob, Roy and Polly said how much they would like to meet Mr Croak, so we decided that we would all go down to the spinney the next day to see if he was there.

The next day, the summer gave us another beautiful sunrise, I was out early and decided to have another poke around in the shed. I quickly found what I was looking for: the book on Boy Scouts. I decided to take it down to the spinney and ask Mr Croak about some of the things in the chapter called Hiking.

Polly found me reading it. "You're planning something," she said poking her head through the window.

"What makes you say that?" I said, quickly shutting the book.

"Cos your tail's going."

"My tail tells all again," I replied. "Come and see this."

"Can we do it later? The others are all waiting at the barn doors."

Goodness, I thought. I must have been sitting, reading in our office for over an hour, the book was that interesting. I stuffed it into a little bag, checked the paper in the machine for that evening's story, closed the cardboard boxes to hide everything; nipped through the window and over the fence to join the others.

"Not like you to be late for an adventure," said Lindy.

"No, I'm sorry," I said. "I got my nose into a book and forgot the time."

Off we trekked across the field. The others had all brought something to eat in little bags which they carried on their backs, and I hoped that Polly had remembered to pack some food for me. Polly took the lead followed by Rob then Roy, with Lindy and then me at the back. We certainly looked an interesting little band, as we wound our way across the back field towards the spinney. Polly turned around and stopped, looking up into the distant sky behind us.

"Look!" she said excitedly and pointed back over the barn. Sure enough, there in the sky above the barn, a black speck appeared in the sky and it was soon joined by a second one. We stood there and watched them as they grew larger and larger until the two storks were right over head. I wondered how on earth they managed to stay in the sky, their large wings flapping up and down so slowly as they flew two big circles above us and then glided down beautifully, disappearing silently over the treetops which lined the spinney.

"Wow!"

"Wow!" said Rob and Roy both together, we all looked at each other and burst out laughing, remembering the fun we had the evening before.

"Come on," said Lindy, "we'll introduce you to Mr Croak and it looks like he's brought a friend along too, what fun."

As we burst out through the bushes onto the bank of the spinney, I spotted Mr Croak and his friend at the far end, standing very quietly with their heads down looking into the water. I told the others to keep very quiet, as lunchtime in the stork world was a serious business and required total silence. It seemed as if the whole spinney was watching and waiting, when suddenly with a double flash both birds whipped a fish each from the water and the spell was broken.

"Ughh!" said Lindy, breaking the silence, "that's the bit I don't like."

Rob and Roy, I could see, were totally impressed. They both stood rigid like musical statues, their mouths agape as the two large birds came up the side of the spinney towards us, their feet, which were on the end of the thinnest, spindliest legs that you've ever seen, not making a sound as they dipped gracefully in and out of the shallow water.

"Good morning," croaked the first stork, lowering his head down on a never-ending neck towards the two little animals.

"G-G-Good M-M-Morning,"

"G-G-Good M-M-Morning," said Rob and Roy together.

"W-W-Why don't you fall over?" said Roy, trying to stand as tall as he could.

The stork laughed and replied, "It's all a question of balance, my brave little friend," and with that we all laughed and made friends.

Mr Croak had brought his brother down to sample their favourite fish, and they strolled back up the spinney to finish their fishing. We all settled down on the bank with our picnic. Polly had thoughtfully packed some lunch for me, and after eating it, I fetched out the Boy Scout book. Lindy and I were soon eagerly flipping through the pages of the book which was full of interesting things like camping and hiking and lots more.

Polly, in the meantime, had hauled in the pirate log and enlisted Rob and Roy as crew; the three of them were having a high old time playing at pirates and Mr Croak and his brother watched on in amusement.

After a while, I thought it was time to get down to business and called out, "Mr Cr...err Stork, could you explain a couple of things I've found in this book?"

"You can call me Sam," replied the bird, "and my brother's name is Sidney."

"Oh! How rude of me," I answered, "this is Lindy, and my sister Polly is on our pirate ship and her two shipmates are Rob and Roy.

"Well, now that we all know one another let's have a look at that book of yours." Sam bent his head down and cleverly flicked the pages over with his long beak, his eyes flashing over each page.

"Interesting," he said looking up at me. "I can only think that you must be planning a long trek, that's what this Boy Scouting lark seems to be about." As I looked back into his wise old eyes, I realised that Sam had discovered my hidden secret almost before I had, and everybody gathered round me on the bank. I couldn't believe myself as I told them all of my plan to hike down to the big river before the end of the summer, it just sort of flowed out without me even thinking.

"You can't go on your own!" squeaked Rob.

"Well, I wasn't thinking of going alone," I replied. "I rather thought that you all would like to come too, you see this book tells us how to do it."

"Oh wow!" cried Polly with excitement, and everybody started chatting excitedly at the same time.

"Hold it! Hold it! Hold it!" said Sam raising his voice and his head above everybody else. "These are serious plans you are making, and I can assure you that, that book does not tell you everything. Gather round and I'll tell you about some of the things you may meet between here and the big river, then you must go home and think hard about what you are planning, and we will meet back here tomorrow to discuss things further."

I was very impressed by this speech, and I realised that Sam Stork was a very wise old bird. I could see that the others also hung on his every word.

Sam told us about the countryside, the woods and forests, lakes and fields, the roads and tracks with their dangerous motor vehicles, and the different animals which we may meet on our journey.

"Did you know that there is a large family of foxes living right next to you in the next field?"

"Yes," replied Lindy, "Rob and Roy have been keeping an eye on them and they seem to be keeping themselves to themselves."

"Then how do you account for two of them watching us from a hiding place, close by, right now." said Sidney.

"What!" exclaimed some of us and, "Where?" shouted the others, all looking around in different directions towards the edge of the spinney.

"You won't see them, but you can bet that they can see you," said Sam quietly with a voice of authority, "But don't be afraid of them, they are mostly just nosey and want to know about everything that's going on. But never trust a fox, they will only worry you if you find yourself on your own. So that's rule number one; always stay together in one group."

"Patrol!" I shouted out loud.

"Ah-Ah!" said Sam. "Still got your nose in that Boy Scout book, I see, Anna."

"Yes," I replied proudly, "they divide themselves up into what's called patrols with a leader and a second in command, and they all have stout willow staves."

"What's a stave?" asked Roy.

"It's a stout stick." I replied, "And you carve your patrol sign and number on it, that should scare off any foxes." I continued raising my voice loudly.

"It may well do," said Sam, "But don't rely on it, always stay together in your patrol and then you'll be safe."

"How do you know that the foxes are watching us now?" asked Polly.

"We saw them stalking you as you came across the back-field, they crept further away when we swooped down and circled round, but you can be sure that they are out there somewhere watching us. Don't worry they've got plenty to eat this time of the year, but as winter approaches, they get a little hungrier and need watching. You must always light a fire at night, that will keep them away, and if you are still sure that you want to take this journey Sidney and I will fly out every day to see that you are all right."

The others all looked at me.

"Yes," I said, not really knowing why I said it. Must be the cat dad in me, I thought, as all the others said yes in their own ways.

"Well," said Sam. "Looks like you've got your patrol leader now who's going to be second in command?"

"Lindy!!" shouted the other three to my great joy. "Now Miss patrol leader, and how are you going to look after your patrol?"

"Well," I replied thoughtfully, "We'll all have our staves, and wet weather clothes, which must be light… weight as well."

"It hasn't rained for ages," said Polly.

"I know," I said. "But autumn is coming, some of the leaves are already turning gold and we can't trust the weather from now on."

"Well said and what else?" said Sam.

"I'll sneak a box of matches from the kitchen and keep them in a waterproof plastic bag and we will all take a good supply of food for six days; three days there and three days back." I looked around at everybody feeling quite pleased with myself.

"That sounds like enough food and enough time for the journey," continued Sam. "Where will you sleep?"

"We'll all take a warm sleeping blanket, and in the book it shows you how to make a little shelter out of small branches and bush called a bivouac."

"You've certainly given this a lot of thought, top marks for your planning, Anna," said Sam, and Sidney nodded in agreement. "Have you anything else up your sleeve?"

"Plenty," I said, "Like how to keep travelling straight by choosing tall trees and keeping them in line behind you as you hike, a bit like how they bring ships into port at night by keeping one light on the land directly behind another."

"H-mmm," said Sam, with a little grin. "That book must be for Sea-Scouts as well, you're not planning on going as far as the seaside, are you?"

"No," I said with a laugh. "But I can also take a piece of mirror and we can signal our position to you each morning; that's if the sun is shining."

"Exactly," replied Sam, becoming much more serious. "If the sun is shining!"

"Your plans are all very well if things are going well, but I want you to try and think what it would be like if the sun wasn't shining. In fact, what it would be like if it was night-time, raining and the rain was slowly putting your fire out. The family of foxes next door will give up following you after a couple of fields, but there will be other animals interested in your strange little patrol as it crosses their territory."

We all looked at each other with dismay.

"Now, don't worry too much about it," continued Sam. "But, before making any big decision, it's always worth looking how bad things may become, instead of how good they might be. As far as the weather is concerned, we will be your eyes in the air and we can see bad weather approaching much easier and sooner than you will, and if things do get a bit wet one of us will stay with you through the night."

"Oh, thank you Mister Sam." we all shouted with relief.

"Well, I don't think that there's anything else we can add," said the stork, "We'll see you here the same time tomorrow."

"Err Sam," I said lowering my voice so the foxes couldn't hear, "I think that, because of the weather the sooner we go the better. As patrol leader I have decided that we leave before dawn tomorrow."

"Okay, we'll see you here at mid-day tomorrow!" said Sam in a very loud voice, and then in a low whisper he said, "Be here at the crack of dawn, that will give us a good start on the foxes, they'll follow your scent for a few fields but soon give up when they get too far away from their den.

With that, the two birds rose slowly into the air and flapped off in the direction of the barn.

We all started back across the field in our patrol order, everybody deep in their own thoughts about the coming adventure. I was in my usual position at the rear of the column, and sure enough, when I sneaked a little look behind us, I saw two red ears duck down out of sight. The foxes, I thought, are more active than Rob and Roy think.

In a loud voice, I said "Remember everybody, tomorrow at mid-day we'll bring up any final questions that we have, with Sam and Sidney and all being well, plan to leave the day after." I immediately stooped down, picked up a large clod of earth, spun round and threw it in the general direction where I had seen the ears. Sure enough, we saw two bushy red tails slipping into the long grass and we could hear their commotion until we saw them disappear into the hedgerow over on the side of the field towards their den.

"Wow!"

"Wow!" said Rob and Roy together, and "Well done," said the other two, patting me on the back. And, as we carried on across the field it occurred to me that, being a patrol leader was a bigger job than I had first thought. The foxes were now well out of earshot, so I began to tell the others, firstly to wrap their food up in something waterproof, and put it in a bag which can be carried in comfort on their backs, the bed-roll should be strapped on top of this and to hang a little cup from the bottom. Rob and Roy were to be in charge of ropes and string and things. I'd bring the matches, mirror and a little old saucepan, Polly and Lindy would bring themselves and anything else they could think of.

In the barn, we found some stout sticks which we decided, made excellent staves, we all said goodnight and, with a promise that we would all meet at the barn doors before dawn the following day, we each went in our different directions home for our last night's sleep in the comfort of our warm beds.

Chapter 6
Discovery

What happened to Polly and I next, was such a big surprise that it nearly put a stop to all our plans. As Polly and I crept through the hole in the fence, we were faced by two pairs of children's shoes, in which were children's feet, and looking up we gazed into the eyes of Holly and Poppy, the two elder children and they both had a very serious look about them.

They bent down and each picked one of us up, Holly walked slowly down the garden with me, Poppy followed close behind with Polly. I began to purr contentedly as Holly lovingly stroked me, but I knew that something was wrong, I had this funny sort of feeling down in my tummy. Holly opened the shed door; we all went inside and Poppy closed the door gently behind us. The girls placed us down gently side by side on the worktop. Polly gave me a worried look and I glanced away to the corner where our cardboard office was hidden. It all looked pretty undisturbed, but my heart was beating fifteen to the dozen.

"Well," said Holly in a quiet voice, "and what have our two brave little cats been up to today pirate ships or aerial…runways?"

I knew then that all our secrets had been discovered. "We think that you are very clever cats," said Poppy, "and I'm afraid that we accidentally found your wonderful little office whilst hunting for the sledge. Winter's coming soon and we thought that we should get it out ready.

"Anyway, we couldn't resist reading your stories," continued Holly, "we didn't realise that you have so many adventures and they do make such exciting reading, we hope you don't mind." She then began to open our cardboard office, "Your magic word machine is actually called a typewriter and it was so clever of you to discover how to use it, we are very proud of you."

Poppy couldn't contain herself any longer, "Yes and now we can be in your story! And could have a go on your aerial runway Polly; and can you teach me how to type Anna, and the spinney and the pirate ship sound great, and oh yes, thanks for the tadpoles and…and…and…

"Hold it! Hold it! Hold it!" cried Holly.

I jumped down onto the magic word machine and quickly tapped out, "You sound just like Sam Croak Holly," and everyone laughed which made us all feel a lot better.

"I'm glad that I do," replied Holly. "He sounds like a very good and wise friend to me, and like us he seems very concerned about this hiking adventure to the big river that you're all planning. What would Mum and Dad say if they knew? They'd certainly start worrying if you didn't come in for tea one evening.

I again typed out. "That one evening will be tomorrow evening and now that you mention it, I feel very guilty and upset about mum and dad and how much they would worry, how absolutely thoughtless of us."

"Oh, don't worry about that," said Poppy excitedly, "Cats often wander off for a time, I heard mum and dad talking only the other day about some cat in the village who disappeared one day; and walked back into the house, as right as rain, a year and a half later expecting its tea to be ready."

"However," continued Holly, "If you animals really mean to go on this adventure, we can't really stop you.

But we will also be worried about you, and we'll do our best to appease mum and dad, but you must tell Sam Croak to circle once round the house each night, on his way home, just to show us that everything is okay.

"We will! We will!" I tapped out happily, realising that our secret was still safe, and that Holly and Poppy were most certainly now a part of our story. How happy it made me feel.

Holly and Poppy promised to get our backpacks ready for the morning and leave them just outside the cat flap.

Chapter 7
A Misty Morning

Polly and I awoke early the following morning, the backpacks were there as promised, and we made our way silently to the barn doors. Lindy was already there, and we were soon joined by Rob and Roy.

The sun had still not risen as we picked up our staves and headed out into the mist which swirled eerily over the backfield. Everything seemed strangely different as we filed slowly across the field towards the spinney. It may have been because it was grey and dark, but deep down inside I knew that it was because we were leaving the safety of our home for the first time, and it gave me a feeling of both sadness and excitement at the same time. I turned back to look towards our house, the light was on in the top room, and I could see two little silhouettes in the yellow square of the window. Holly and Poppy; and they were waving. I turned to look back a few times, but the window turned into a fuzzy glow as we walked further into the mist and then was gone.

The mist made everything appear grey and menacing.

Polly, who was leading suddenly stopped and we all bumped into each other, "What is it?" I whispered, and

Polly pointed to a large grey shape moving slowly across our path. We all froze to the spot, our heartbeats thumping in our throats.

"I think it's my aunt Lucinda, out for her early morning stroll," said Lindy with relief, and sure enough, we could hear the chomp, chomp, chomp of aunt Lucinda's teeth as she disappeared off into the greyness, the chomping noise was there but Aunt Lucinda had vanished as we crept on past towards the spinney.

The grey outline of the hedgerow loomed out of the mist in front of us, we soon found our little hole and we all crept through it onto the bank of the spinney.

"Whew, so far so good," said Polly. "That was a ghostly scare back then." We all agreed, and I looked round at our patrol, they all seemed in good spirits.

"Good morning," came a voice from the mist, "Good to see you all up early," It was Sam stork standing in the gloom at the end of the spinney.

"Good morning to you Sam," replied Polly. "How did you land in the dark?"

"Ah, I spent the night here," said Sam, "I flew back here before dark. Are you all ready?"

"Yes," I said in my best patrol-leader voice. "All packed and ready to go. The Barn Door Patrol at your service.

"The Barn Door Patrol Eh?" said Sam, "and a braver little team I've yet to see. Well, here's our plan. As you know, the early start is to leave the spinney before the foxes are up. So straight away we'll skirt round the spinney and go out through a gap in the hedgerow on the far side under that large oak tree."

We all turned to look in the direction of Sam's beak and looking out of the rising mist we saw the shadow of the oak. Off we set, keeping our usual positions, Sam striding along beside us in the shallows. When we reached the gap, Sam stopped us, "Now if you follow the track keeping that hedge you see on your left: after about fifteen minutes you will cross a farm-track, keeping the hedgerow to your left you'll follow the track which skirts around the back of the farm to a lake on the other side. I'll meet you there in about an hour, it's beginning to get light so that will help. Now off you go before the foxes are up and about."

We walked briskly along the path, in silence and soon covered the distance to the track. We knew we were there well before we arrived, for we heard a low rumbling sound which gradually grew into a loud roar, and the bright lights of a tractor and trailer flashed across in the mist ahead lighting up the end of the hedgerow for a few seconds and then all returned to misty grey again, the lights and the noise receding into the distance.

We stopped at the edge of the farm-track, looked in both directions, skipped across to pick up our path on the other side and continued to skirt around the back of the farm. Through the hedge, we could see the dull light of the farm buildings and we heard the sounds of the farm as it came to life for another day. The tractor lights went back the other way, in the gloom behind us shouts of men calling to each other, the sudden bark of a dog uncomfortably near. We all stopped dead still.

"Did you hear that bark?" said Polly, up front. "It sounded very much like a fox to me." And before she had finished, there was another bark much nearer.

"Quick! Into the bushes," I whispered, and we all crept quietly into the hedgerow and waited not making a sound. There followed another bark which seemed further off and then nothing.

"It's only a farm dog," I said. "They must have let him out for his morning wee. Come on we've got to get to the lake in time for Sam."

So, off we went again the farm noises disappearing behind us.

It was a strange feeling, being far away from home, and I was just wondering why we were attempting this adventure, when the answer appeared before me.

All along the hedgerow, the birds began to sing their dawn chorus as the sky beyond took on a pale-yellow glow. Dawn was arriving and, in the distance, it could be heard. Our spirits rose with the mist as the sun lit up the treetops with a flash of golden colour. A flight of ducks swooped down over our heads, as if to welcome us, and disappeared between the trees. We could hear the splashes as they landed on the lake, another bird hooted off to our right, and we walked through the tree line to see the most beautiful expanse of water disappearing to our left and right and off into the distance as far as the eye could see, directly in front and below us stood a forest of bull-rushes their soft brown heads swaying in a natural dance to the early morning breeze.

In the middle distance, lay an island and I could pick out two white flashes in the water; swans. "Swan Island," I whispered in true wonder, and the others smiled at each other overcome by the absolute beauty of the place.

"Wow!" said Roy, "can we find a pirate log and sail out there?"

"I shouldn't think so," replied Lindy. "That island looks like it belongs to those swans. I wouldn't like to go near it. Swans can get pretty hissy when they are angry; any way, we have to stick to our plan, or we'll never reach the big river."

"That's right! And good to see you." Croaked Sam stork his head popping up on the other side of the bull-rushes. "How was your hike round the farm?"

"The farm was well awake," piped in Polly, "Noisy tractors, barking dogs and the farm men calling to one another, but this is so beautiful and peaceful it was well worth the walk."

"Yes, it's one of my favourite places," went on Sam. "I call it Swan Lake. Those two out there on the island have lived here as long as I can remember. Every year, they breed another family on the island and every year, in the early autumn, their offspring return to the island bringing their cygnets with them. Four weeks ago, there must have been close to fifty swans out there having a right old get together, but they've all flown back to their own homes for the winter leaving old Ma and Pa with their latest brood. There's four of them and very fine birds they are too. I swear they get better each year. The two young ones must be round the other side of the island.

The word winter brought me back to earth, and I waited until Sam had finished before saying quietly, "Yes, it's a truly wonderful place, but which way do we go from here? We seem to have lost our stream. It must run into the lake somewhere near here."

"Your stream swung in a big loop around the other side of the farm. If we walk along the lakeside towards the sun, we shall find where it runs into the lake. We'll stop there and have our breakfast."

We started off along the side of the lake. "Do you mean that our little stream fills this huge lake?" asked Rob in amazement.

"It helps," replied Sam from the other side of the bulrushes, but there are four other streams flowing into it at different points round the top side, down at the bottom end there's only one going out, it falls over a waterfall, down there to the right of that church spire you can see, and then wanders off across the field in the direction of the big river. We'll be around there tonight and that's where we'll make camp.

"How exciting," said Lindy, and we all agreed.

As we walked on towards our breakfast spot the bulrushes led onto a green bank of grass edged with a sandy beach running along the lakeside. Sam finally joined us, splashing along in the shallows at our side. It felt very safe with Sam around.

We soon arrived at the place where the spinney stream joined the lake. The stream was pretty low due to the lack of rain and just a small trickle flowed into the lake. There was a sturdy bridge which indicated that the water rose quite high at times. We crossed over the bridge and sat down on the grass bank on the other side. Everybody was hungry and tucked into their food in silence.

I discovered a little folded note at the bottom of my bag, it was from Poppy and Holly wishing us good luck and to come home safe and soon. I showed it to Poppy, and she immediately dived to the bottom of her bag. To her delight there was another note from the children, saying, that Sam; our dog, Digger and Buttercup, the rabbits, Honey, the hamster, the goldfish, Mr Toad and his family, the squirrel family that lived in the roof above the toy-room, the doves and the sheep in the back-field all sent their best wishes and all the luck in the world. We sat in the warm sun thinking of all our friends back home.

"I hope that everyone is keeping an eye on their food, and not eating it-all at once," I said. "We don't want to run out. In case we do, I want you, Lindy, to look for things on the way that we can pick to eat. I've got the saucepan and there will always be water close at hand, if we keep to the streams and lakes."

"Right oh," replied Lindy.

I then got onto another important subject that had been puzzling me. "When we finally arrive back home," I said to everybody, "I've got to write about our adventures on the magic word machine and I can't think of an easy way to remember everything. The only way is to give each person a day each and when we get home, it's up to each person to remember what happened on the allotted day. So, what I want to do is this: there's five of us and I estimate that we'll be gone for six days. I'll take days one and six, Rob and Roy you take days two and three, Polly day four and Lindy day five; that should cover everything." There was silence whilst everyone thought about my suggestion. Then Rob stood up. "I think I may have a better idea," he said, and Sam stork cocked his head sideways towards Rob in order to hear better.

"Good," I said, "we need all the ideas we can get. What is it, Rob?"

"Well," he started slowly, "you know that you could never write like the children and the grown-ups, because you couldn't hold the pencil correctly in your paws, and Lindy neither. Well, Roy and me, we tried it and we can do it. We can't write of course but we can draw pretty good pictures, we've got different hands to you see," he said holding up his two little claws.

"Any way I've got paper, pencils, a pencil sharpener and a rubber in my bag and Roy and me will draw little pictures each evening of that day's adventures; what do you think?"

"I think that's splendid!" spoke up Sam, "what ingenious little chaps you are." And we all clapped Rob and Roy on their backs, because they were clever and always came up with good ideas.

"That's great, I promote you to official patrol reporters, and when we get home, you can draw the actual pictures to go in the book."

"Three cheers for Rob and Roy," shouted Polly and the two rats sat there as pleased as a punch whilst we danced around them with joy, Sam stork looking on and nodding his head in agreement.

When the celebration had died down, I decided that we should pack everything away in our bags and clear the bank of any signs that we had been there.

Whilst the others were tidying up, I strolled over to Rob and Roy. "That was a great surprise," I said, "Have you any pictures with you?"

Roy dug into his knapsack and produced a plastic waterproof folder; he opened it and pulled some sheets of paper out. "There's Sam stork, and here's Rob and me on the aerial runway and here's you asleep under the blue bush."

I looked at the pictures with interest, the one of Sam swooping down out of the sky was very good, and I must admit they had caught my likeness very well.

"These are terrific," I said, "How long have you been drawing?"

"Well, you remember back in the summer when we used to play on the aerial runway with Polly and you and Lindy would disappear off over the spinney to chat all afternoon," said Roy.

"Yes," I said.

"Well, Rob and me sneaked into Holly and Poppy's bedroom one day and found the paper, pencils, rubber and sharpener. We only meant to borrow them you see, but I'm afraid that we've borrowed them for a longer time than we first thought."

"I'm sure that Holly and Poppy won't mind," I replied. "Especially when they see the pictures that you will draw. In fact, they will both probably want to sit for their portraits." Rob and Roy chuckled at the idea, and, packing their artists' materials away, they found their positions in the patrol and we were all set to go.

I gave a last look around to see if we had left any telltale clues and finding nothing, we set off along the rough path which clung to the side of the lake. Sam told us that it was mostly used by animals and the odd fisherman. It curved round the top corner of the lake and we were soon heading along at a good pace with the rising sun to our left and the lake on our right. Soon Sam left us to fly ahead and check on our evening campsite.

We made good progress; there was lots to see, and lots of noises which we couldn't identify coming from the line of reeds which edged the lake. Roy spotted a very large fish with ferocious looking teeth, rise out of the water a little way out from the bank. He said that it gave him an 'I could eat you for my dinner,' look, but by the time he managed to shout to us, all we saw was a large ring of swirls where the fish had vanished back into the deeps.

We disturbed the occasional coot and moorhen but they were all pretty friendly. On the other side of the path, there seemed to be a lot of interest in us, lots of scurrying noises in the hedgerow but never anything to actually see.

One thing that disturbed me a little, were three crows which flew overhead, circled us and flew off in the same direction at least six times during the morning. It was as if they were reporting back our position to somebody.

Chapter 8
Walt and Will

We stopped on another grassy bank for some lunch, a bit tired and very hot. The sun had climbed to its full height, and we all had our coats slung over our backpacks by mid-day and were very glad to lay about in the comfort of the grass and open up our lunch.

Lindy had been busy on the way, and, with some help from Polly and the two rats, had collected a fair-sized bag of sweet chestnuts, blackberries, hazelnuts and conkers. "We'll have those with our supper," I said.

"But I don't think I'll be having conkers for pudding." There were lots of squeaky sounds and plops coming from the water's edge, so Rob and Roy decided to go and investigate. As I watched them creep through the long grass to the water's edge, I looked further on down the side of the lake and spotted what looked like Sam and Sidney flopping slowly towards us low over the water.

As Rob and Roy reached the reeds the noises stopped, but as they started examining the reeds more closely, a little way along the bank, up popped two little heads almost identical to theirs.

"Hallo."

"Hallo," said Rob and Roy, shocked into their old double-talking habit.

"Hallo."

"Hallo," replied the two little heads.

"What you doin'?"

"What you doin'?"

"Are you making fun of us?"

"Are you making fun of us?" went on Rob and Roy.

"No, but what are you doin'?"

"No, but what are you doin'?" repeated the two little water rats, because that was most certainly what the two newcomers were.

"Why aren't you in the water? It's lovely in."

"Why aren't you in the water? It's lovely in."

The two barn rats having shaken off their initial surprise, reverted back into normal speech and Roy explained that they were just out for a stroll with their friends and that they were barn rats not water rats and couldn't really swim.

"Well, you should learn, you don't know what you're missing. Anyway, there's not a barn for miles. What's your names? And who are your friends and what are you doing and where are you going?" said one of the water rats also reverting back to normal speech. This speech thing must be common to all sets of twin rats I thought, and they certainly want to know a lot too.

"Robert and Royston, why what's yours?"

"Walter and William, but you can call us Walt and Will if you like.

"Oh well you can call us Rob and Roy then," continued Roy in a friendlier manner, and the four of them started a friendly argument about which life was better water or barn, until finally Roy said, "Okay then who is the big ugly fish and is he a friend of yours?"

"Did it have teeth and look like it would have you for dinner?" asked Will.

"Yes," said Roy.

"That's Percy Pike. He's the biggest in the lake, there's a family of them that live in the deep, out in the middle. We haven't seen him over here, near the bank all summer. He must have come over to check who you were and what you are up to. He'd eat you if he could get you. We stay well clear of him. The ducks and coots and other animals soon give plenty of warning whenever he comes snooping around.

I noticed that Rob and Roy had not given anything away about our expedition, which was very clever of them.

Suddenly, the two water rats shot back into the reeds leaving a surprised Rob in mid-sentence.

The reason was soon quite obvious, for Sam and Sidney came swooping in to land at the water's edge, both birds immediately standing stock still, their eyes pointing down towards the water's surface.

"Do you two fish all the time?" I shouted out.

"No, but it's always worth checking out a new patch on arrival," said Sam.

After spearing a few fish for a quick snack, the two birds strode over to the bank and called us all to a meeting.

"The lake's pretty low," said Sam, "there's just a trickle over the water-fall at the dam. The evening campsite looks okay. How are you all for food?"

Everybody said that they had plenty left and Lindy and Polly showed them the bag full of nuts and berries.

"Very good," said Sam. "You may need them later, keep collecting anything eatable on the way."

Sam took me aside and I could tell that he was worried about something.

"There's a few things," he said in his gruff voice.

"Firstly, this hot sun is here to stay for some days yet, the lower stream is down to a trickle, and it doesn't look good, we'll have to carry extra water tomorrow, have you enough bottles?"

I said that I had told everyone to bring spare bottles. "The other thing is, that I'm a bit concerned about the crows."

"Oh," I replied. "The three that I have been seeing on and off all day today."

"They were not the same three you kept seeing," went on Sam with a worried look, "but different flights of birds sent out to keep tracks on you. They all fly off in the same direction towards Wood-on-the-Hill which lays in the distance over to our left. Sidney and I flew down there to have a look. We didn't go too close, but from where we were, we could see that the sky above the trees was thick with crows. I've got a strange feeling that something is cooking and it's not nice. We'll camp at the dam tonight, and it's your choice whether you want to go on tomorrow or head back for home. Press on for the dam now and when you arrive, I suggest that you have a serious talk with the others. Sidney is going to have another cruise down towards Wood-on-the-Hill, I'm going back to signal to Holly and Poppy as we promised. We'll all meet at the dam and talk later."

59

Chapter 9
Percy Pike

Sam and Sidney flew off in opposite directions and I mustered the patrol for our hike to the dam.

"What was Sam saying?" asked Polly. "He looked a bit worried."

"Oh nothing," I replied. "He was concerned about our food supplies, but I told him that we had enough."

"We have, if Lindy and I keep gathering the nuts and berries, what do you say to nice hot nut and berry soup tonight?" she said, skipping off to join Lindy.

"Sounds great," I said thoughtfully.

We trekked on through the rest of the afternoon, and by the time we reached the dam, the sun had turned into a big orange ball. We all sat on the grass bank and watched as it descended towards its reflection in the surface of the lake. Nothing could be more beautiful, the waterfowl were busying themselves around the rushes, ducks were flying in for the night, breaking the sun's reflection up into a thousand golden sparkles as they skidded down onto the surface of the lake. Walt and Will had swum down with us, and all four rats had found a nice big pirate log, they were busy banging a mooring post into the bank and hitching a length of rope to it.

Polly, Lindy and I sat in the grass discussing the evening meal.

The rats finally pushed their boat out and pulled it back to the bank. It was pretty sturdy and looked a more formidable pirate ship than our spinney log. It took the four of them easily and looked very stable. They all shouted out various sea-faring phrases, as they pushed the log out with their hiking staves. "Push off, good'n'ard, bowman," "Boom coming over," and "Let's splice the mainbrace," amongst others. It occurred to me that they had all completely forgotten about Percy Pike and I shouted out to them.

"Oh, he goes home when the sun goes down, he doesn't like cold water," shouted back Will.

But unfortunately, today Percy had other ideas.

As I watched the log reach the end of its string, a strange thing happened, or should I say two strange things.

Beyond the boat, I noticed a sudden swirl in the water and Percy Pike leapt out of the water landing with a mighty splash in a shower of golden droplets. The rats also saw this but from a much nearer viewpoint and poor Rob fell overboard with fright. At the same time, I saw about ten black specks flying towards us out of the sun…Crows, I thought that this is getting a bit serious.

The water rats had dived into the water and were busy dragging Rob towards the log. Rob was learning to swim pretty fast, splashing about and swallowing a lot of lake. Meanwhile, Percy's wake circled round the log getting nearer and nearer. He was after his dinner, and he looked hungry.

The three of us ran down to the mooring post and grabbed hold of the rope. Out on the lake, Will and Wilt reached the log and thrust Rob aboard, jumping on themselves just as the big fish arrived at the log giving it such a large thump that they all nearly fell off again.

By this time, the crows were overhead and began to swoop down on our chums, who bravely swiped at the air with their staves.

"Hold tight!" I screamed out, and they all flung themselves flat on the log.

"Pull!" I shouted to Polly and Lindy, and we all pulled as hard as we could and ran up the grassy bank.

The log shot across the water like a speed boat, Percy gave chase whilst the crows dived to the attack. We didn't stop running until we had dragged the log out of the water and well up the grass bank, the four rats tumbled onto the grass and the three of us ran back down towards them, waving our staves and throwing stones at the crows. A lucky shot hit the biggest crow on the head, and he beat off low across the lake with a 'Squark! Squark! Squark!' He must have been the leader because the others followed after him. It was then that I noticed that some of them were magpies. Strange, I thought as they followed the big crow across the lake and all turned in the direction of the Wood-on-the-Hill magpies and crows ganging up together—very strange, and I stood and listened to the 'Wark! Wark!' of the crows and the laughing chatter of the magpies as they died away into the distance.

Chapter 10
The Willow Tree

Percy had also disappeared, and the lakeside was at peace again, as if nothing had ever happened, a sudden shiver ran down my spine. It's certainly beautiful out in the wild, but danger is never far away either. In future, we'll have to be more on our guard. Those birds are definitely a worry, old Sam was right again.

The others were all down with the pirate crew, a very shaken up pirate crew. Rob was still coughing up water, somebody had thrown a warm coat round his shoulders. Polly was congratulating Walt and Will on the rescue and Lindy and Roy were collecting sticks for a fire.

As I walked down to join them, Lindy called out, "Have you got a light for this fire, Anna? I think it's about time, I brewed up that nut and berry soup. I know one pirate that could do with some and I'm pretty hungry myself after that skirmish."

"Good idea," I said giving her the matchbox. "Don't waste any," I said, and Lindy lit the fire with the first try.

"I managed to find these mushrooms this afternoon," said Polly, producing a large pile of lovely white caps from her bag. We can pop them into the soup as well. I checked them out in your Boy Scout Book Anna.

That book is a real treasure, I thought and as I watched our little team busying themselves around the campsite, a sense of pride came over me. The way everyone acted, when faced with a real danger that afternoon, was a credit to them, and now after the event, they were all mucking in together and finding a hidden strength to cope with the nasty scare we had had. Very brave, I thought but underneath, I knew we were all shaken up.

We sat Rob down in the crook of a cosy log, next to the fire and whilst Lindy brewed up her 'lake broth' as she called it, we all unrolled the sleeping bags and made camp. We found some bread in our bags which went very nice with the soup and sat around the fire enjoying the delicious warm soup whilst I told the others of Sam Croak's suspicions concerning the birds.

"Crows and magpies!" squeaked Roy. "Seems a very strange partnership to me."

"Do you think that they sent some kind of message to Percy Pike as well?" said Polly, excitedly.

"That's a bit hard to believe," I replied. "But it certainly seems that there are good guys and bad guys out here in the wild, and at the moment the bad guys have gone, and we're left with the good guys," and turning to Walt and Will I said, "I don't know how to thank you two enough for rescuing Rob this afternoon. He would have certainly been Percy Pike's dinner if it hadn't been for your brave efforts."

"All in an afternoon's work," said Will.

"Lovely soup, Lindy," said Walt.

"Hurray for Will and Walt," shouted Polly, and we all gathered around and thanked them in real barn patrol fashion.

"So, what are you doing out here?" said Walt, "far from your cosy homes."

"We're off to find out where our stream joins the big river," said Polly, "Wanna come?"

The others all looked at me, I looked at Polly with a frown, but it soon changed to a smile when I realised that everyone wanted Walt and Will to join our patrol. "Polly, you really must learn how to keep a secret," I said to my sister, "Even more so out here in the wild. However," I continued, turning to the two water rats, "It seems that our patrol has unanimously voted you in, and we'd love to have you with us if you would like to come. It's pretty clear that we would benefit from your knowledge of the wild; what do you say?"

Walt and Will stood up together, "Yes please," said Will.

"Rather," followed Walt, "We love adventuring, and you certainly need somebody with you who knows the countryside."

So that was that, our patrol was now seven strong. Walt and Will were given the positions of team trackers and so we all sat there whilst dusk descended on our little campsite and waited for Sam and Sidney to return.

We didn't have to wait long, and when they did arrive, everybody started to talk at once.

"Quiet!" I snapped, rather more sternly than I had intended, and all the patrol fell silent.

"What's happened?" asked Sam, so I stood up and gave a short but accurate account of all that had happened since we last saw them.

"Right," said Sam, when I had finished, "Even more reason to have a serious talk and definitely time for some decisions. You're two brave recruits, bring your number up to seven, but that is nothing compared to what you may meet in the wild."

A stern look came over his face as he said this and he continued, "Anna, have you discussed with the others what you intend to do? My advice is to turn around and head back for home; there's something big happening over at Wood-on-the-Hill, Sidney and I haven't got to the bottom of it yet, but it doesn't look good."

I stood up as tall as I could, and began, "We've been talking about what to do for quite a while now and have come to a united decision, but you may have more information which may change that decision.

"I'm afraid that Sidney and I do not know much more than you at the moment," said Sam. "There's something happening over at Wood-on-the-Hill and it's to do with the crows and magpies. I'm not sure whether the nasties like the foxes, stoats and weasels are involved and we haven't managed to contact the nice guys yet, the badgers sleep all day, and the squirrels, rabbits and others seem to have gone to ground… I don't like it."

"Is what's happening a direct result of our expedition?" I asked.

"No, I don't think it is," replied Sam. "The crows have been up to something for some time now, but it's only recently that they have used the magpies for scouting, and I also saw some rooks flying over towards Wood-on-the-Hill."

"Well then I think that our decision is to press on," I said. "Maybe the log thing this afternoon was just a friendly warning. I know that they are keeping an eye on us, but so would anybody if they spotted a strange band crossing their lands."

"Well, all I can say is that you are a very brave band," said Sam, and Sidney nodded in agreement. "So, if that is your final decision, and I cannot dissuade you from it, we'd better talk about your destination for tomorrow evening's campsite."

"You will continue to follow the stream south, and will notice, in the distance to your left, a hill crowned with trees, this is Wood-on-the-Hill. Keep the stream on your right and halfway through the afternoon you will reach the outskirts of a small village. You should skirt around the village as we don't want any trouble with humans. The stream drops into another lake on the other side of the village; make for the far end of the lake where it is ideal for a campsite. It's going to be even hotter tomorrow, so make sure you fill those spare bottles before you leave. Sidney and I will try to find out more about the crows. I will be gone all day and Sidney will fly back at intervals and check that you're alright. I've already reported back to Holly and Poppy so let's settle down and get as much rest as possible—who knows what surprises tomorrow holds?"

We slept an exhausted sleep that night and were all up and packed before light, we filled our bottles and checked our food supplies. Not a lot was left, so we warmed up some soup and had a hearty breakfast.

Walt and Will were elected to join Polly and Lindy on food gathering. They fell in line behind Rob and Roy, and after a brief chat with Sam and Sidney, we climbed down the side of the dam, and picking up the trickle which was our stream, followed its dry bed across a field of tall grass. By the time we had crossed the first field, the light of dawn lit up the silhouette of Wood-on-the-Hill in the distance to the left of our path. Even at this distance, I thought that I could see a smoky cloud over the tops of the trees—the crows, I thought, and gave a little shudder.

All through the morning, we trekked on, the Wood-on-the-Hill slowly moved round the horizon until it was almost directly to our left and still a long way away. The sun climbed the sky and heated up the day. By mid-day, we were exhausted, the stream was now a dried-up bed and we had drunk over half of our water supply. We reached the shadow of a large weeping willow tree and flopped down in the cool grass beneath.

I must have only slept for about an hour, when I was roused from a lovely dream about the blue bush at home, it was Polly who was shaking me and I woke up with a jump to find myself under the beautiful willow tree, feeling cool and refreshed.

All the others were awake and chatting amongst themselves. It seemed that the tree had given us back our strength and we were all eager to press on without any more delay.

"Is nobody hungry?" I said, and nobody was.

"Thirsty?" I asked; no, and definitely not tired anymore; how wonderfully strange.

As we walked along, I realised that we hadn't seen a crow all morning, and looking over towards Wood-on-the-hill I noticed that there was no sign of the cloud of birds that I had seen earlier. I mentioned this to Lindy, "Maybe it was all a bad dream," she said. "Sometimes, at home I would dream that I was being chased by a fox, and would wake up, my feet pounding away into my mum's belly. She didn't mind and soon calmed me down and cheered me up again, a bit like that big old willow tree back there.

"Talking of home," I said, "Did you tell your mum where you were going to? I'm sure she wouldn't have agreed to it."

"No, you're right," replied Lindy. "But I did tell my Aunt Lucinda, she's much more worldly-wise and I knew that she would tell mum, but in her own way so as not to worry mum too much."

"Ah, and that's why Aunt Lucinda was out early chomping, when we were leaving."

"Yes," continued Lindy, "she said she'd see us off. She'll laugh when I tell her about the fright she gave us."

The mention of home brought a feeling of nostalgia, but it soon disappeared. However, it did also remind me about our book, and I asked Lindy to take up the rear position whilst I had a chat with Rob and Roy.

"Rob-Roy!" I said, and they both swung their heads around at the same time. Things have been happening so quickly that I was wondering if you've had the time to keep up with the pictures? Our book is going to make really exciting reading if we can remember everything that has happened.

"Oh yes," said Roy. "We're getting very quick; we've come up with the idea of dividing the sheet of paper into twelve squares and doing quick little sketches a bit like a comic. Look," he said, pulling the latest sheet out of his bag. "We call it our storyboards, we're both doing one so that we don't miss anything," added Rob.

"That's great," I said, noticing that the last picture on both storyboards was the beautiful willow tree. "That willow tree, we'll have to make into a feature picture in our book," I said.

"Yes, it seemed to have a lasting effect on all of us," said Roy.

We pressed on through the afternoon and the effect that the willow tree had on us gradually wore off, and by the time that the village church spire showed between the trees we were all feeling very hungry.

Polly, Will and Wilt reported full bags of nuts, berries and mushrooms, in fact, realising how important food collecting was. Everybody had their own bag full, and we were all looking forward to a well-earned feast.

"We'll eat when we've skirted the village," I said. "Polly, look for a path to our left we'll skirt around the village and join the riverbed on the other side."

Chapter 11
Mimsy's Gang

Polly had just turned back to lead the way, when a black and white kitten jumped out of the bushes onto the path a little way in front of her.

"Stand and deliver, you're surrounded!" he said, waving a sword stick in the air. I turned around, and sure enough, we were surrounded; a larger ginger cat stood in the middle of the track which we had just walked up.

"Where you goin'?" said the kitten, still shaking his sword at us.

Polly, seeing the chance of some fun, replied, "We come in peace from the lands beyond Swan Lake and seek your permission to travel across your patch."

"Wow, really, but where are you going?" said the kitten, lowering his sword and looking at the patrol in awe.

Meanwhile, the ginger cat had strolled up behind Lucy and me and said casually, "Hello, I'm Ginger Tom. Don't pay too much attention to Patchy, he sometimes gets a bit theatrical. Follow us, we'll take you to Mimsy; she'll know what to do. Don't worry about the humans, everybody's gone to the cricket match." As we followed the two cats into the deserted village, it occurred to me that it must be Sunday.

Mimsy was a large fluffy white Persian who lived in a Georgian house on the east side of the village. She lay on a crimson cushion in the bay window and being ushered into her presence was a bit like being summoned before the queen.

"Hey, Mimsy!" shouted Patch, as we entered the plush lounge. "Get a load of these guys, they're really cool. In fact, they're so cool I think I may join them."

"Don't be so tiresome, Patch," purred the white cat with an air of detached sophistication. "You can't even join a piece of string. Anyway, what are they up to?" she purred on, giving us a long inquisitive stare. This made us feel rather uncomfortable having interrupted her Sunday afternoon siesta.

"They haven't told us yet, but I bet it's cool; get a load of the rats and the sheep," went on Patch, with excitement.

"I think that what Patchy is trying to get over Mims," put in Ginger, "is that they appear to be a very strange group, and, to my way of thinking, any strange group has got to be up to something pretty strange. Wouldn't you agree?"

"Oh, do cut the dribble, Ginger," went on Mimsy, stepping two rungs down the aristocratic ladder and showing a little more of the alley cat. "Let's hear their story, and then maybe we can help them. By the way, where's Marmite and Wellington, I haven't seen them since lunch?"

"They've gone over to the cricket match," put in Patch. "You know, they'd die for a bloater paste sandwich and Marmite said that smoked salmon is on today, it must be a cup match."

"Oh dear," sighed Mimsy. "All my efforts trying to groom those two girls for high society, suddenly dashed by a bloater sandwich."

"I say, the smoked salmon sounds a bit tasty. I think I might just wander over myself," said Ginger to nobody in particular and sidled off towards the lounge door.

Our patrol, it seemed, had been totally forgotten during this general domestic patter, but Mimsy turned to us and said to Ginger in a more commanding tone, "Yes, Ginger, you mosey on down there, but don't scoff it all yourself, bring plenty back for our guests especially some bloater sandwiches," she added, licking her lips, "and anything else you can lay your hands on. If I'm not mistaken this strange band of ours look like they're on some sort of an expedition and I bet they're starving."

I was taking a liking to Mimsy, who then added, "Get Marmite and Wellington to help you back with a few sack loads. We'll make up a hamper; I mean some travelling packs for their journey."

"Anything you say old thing," simpered Ginger.

"Oh, and don't arouse the humans. You tend to get on the clumsy side when you're hungry."

"Certainly, my sweet, is there anything else?

"We're a bit partial to a piece of walnut and carrot cake, if there's any going," piped up Roy.

"Don't push your luck ratty or I might have you for my dinner," muttered Ginger under his breath.

"What did you say, Ginger?" asked Mimsy.

"I said that I'd see what was available, my love." And with that he disappeared with Patch around the lounge door.

"Now," she said, directing her gaze at me, "You look serious enough to be the leader. What's your name and kindly tell me what you're up to, trekking across our manor?"

I firstly introduced everybody and went on to tell her about our journey to the big river and the adventures we had had on the way so far. I was careful not to mention our book nor the magic word machine.

"Well, well, well...you are a busy bunch and brave too, by all accounts. Those crows certainly sound like a mean lot, I must say that I've noticed that there's a few more about than usual just recently, I wonder what they can be up to, and magpies; dear me, so common, and they take to stealing I'm told."

"Yes, ma'am," cut in Lindy, "But, begging your pardon, we must press on soon. You see, we have to meet Sam and Sidney Stork at the lake just south of the village, before sunset and it's getting a bit lateish."

"Yes, Sam and Sidney are a great help to you, I can see that," purred on Mimsy. "But don't worry, after the cricket match, they always eat tea at 4.30 PM promptly, the others will return soon. We'll feast you up and escort you safely out of the village by six. The sun doesn't set until 8.00 PM; in the meantime, why don't you find yourselves a nice cushion each and take a little snooze."

Sure enough, after about half an hour, we heard the unmistakable tone of Ginger's voice, trying to keep some order. He was hustling the three kittens up the garden path, each one laden down with a bag of leftovers from the cricket match. Ginger strolled through the door with the other three panting behind him.

"Ginger, you really shouldn't work yourself so hard," said Mimsy, sarcastically.

"Oh, it's no trouble really, Mims," replied Ginger, failing to spot the sarcasm.

The three kittens spread the food out on the lounge floor, and it certainly looked great. We hadn't eaten since breakfast and immediately started tucking in. There was even walnut and carrot cake, much to Rob and Roy's delight.

When we had eaten our fill, the three kittens helped us to pack the remains of the meal into our bags.

Mimsy beckoned me up beside her, in the bay window and chatted away to me for some time. Apparently, her mother was brought up in a large mansion down near the big river, and she still had many relatives in the region. She rather fancied coming along with us to visit a few of them, but that she wasn't one for trekking.

She finally took on a more serious expression, and turning to the three kittens, who were now playing a game of hide and seek with Polly and the rats, she snapped kindly, "Come on you three, the party's over for now. You've got to escort our friends down to the lake. Give the village green a wide berth; go through churchyard and across the spinney to Badger wood. You shouldn't bump into any humans that way, only the vicar and he's no trouble; oh, and fill your bottles at the tap in the garden before you leave."

The mention of the spinney made me feel homesick for a minute, but the feeling soon vanished. We said our

75

thanks to Mimsy for her hospitality and with promises to pop in on the way back, we followed Ginger and the kittens out of the room, through the kitchen and out into the garden. By the time we reached Mimsy's window, she was asleep on her cushion. However, as I reached the gate, I turned for one last look, she opened her eyes and gave me a big wink, I waved and slipped around the gatepost to catch up with the others.

At the end of the lane, Ginger wandered off on his own. He turned and wished us good luck and was gone. We were left with Patch, Wellington and Marmite, who still thought it was great fun, I tried to get them to keep the noise down, but they chattered all the way to Badger's Wood.

As we walked through the trees, I noticed how the leaves were mostly turned to gold. Autumn, but still so hot during the day, and still no rain, I thought as I heard the village church bell chime seven in the distance behind us.

At the edge of the wood, we looked down across the fields. "Look," said Patch, "The stream follows that line of willow trees, and if you follow it along the lake, it is just beyond the tree line where those two large birds are circling." I looked just in time to make out the shapes of Sam and Sidney as they disappeared over the trees by the lake. What a comfort they were, I thought, our only link with home.

"Okay guys, stay cool," said Patch, back in his play-acting role, and then turning to Polly he drew out his swordstick and offered it to her handle first.

"Take this dear friend," he said in a serious tone. "And may it both defend you and remind you of me, at all times." He bowed low and Polly took the sword.

"I will return it to you on our way back," she said, "and we'll have another party. When's the next cricket match?" We all laughed and clapped, but I could see that Polly and Patch had made a special bond with each other.

We strode off down through the long grass towards the line of willow trees, and upon reaching them turned to wave goodbye to the three kittens. They were still there, caught in the gold of the late sun. They turned, and with a last wave from Patch disappeared into the shadows of Badgers Wood.

It was good to meet up with Sam and Sidney again. To tell them of our day's adventures and to share the remains of the wonderful food with them. "Here," I said, digging deep into my bag, "Try this," and I pulled out four lovely pieces of smoked-salmon which I had saved especially for them.

"I say," croaked Sam, "How the rich live? You must have been mixing with the aristocracy."

I think we have, I thought to myself as I watched Sam and Sidney enjoying the fish I had given them.

I remembered seeing a large house near the big river in one of Holly's books at home. It was called something like Hampton Court, where kings and queens once lived, and I had made my mind up that that was the house Mimsy was referring to, definitely aristocracy. "Another bloater paste sandwich, Sidney, old boy?" Roy was saying to a rather full Sidney.

"I'm not sure I can take another one," replied Sidney in his poshest voice, but he gobbled it up just the same.

After we had finished eating and everything was cleared away, we spread out our packs and crawled into them tired and full. Sam and Sidney then explained what they had been doing during the day.

"I flew over towards Wood-on-the-Hill," said Sam, pointing his long beak in the direction of the hilltop which could still be seen picked out in gold on the distant horizon. "As I approached, I saw some crows heading out in my direction, so I flew up high above their range. When I arrived over the hilltop, it all seemed pretty quiet, and I found out why later. I met a rook, an old friend of mine. He won't have any part of this crow thing but what he did say was that they've crowned a King Crow, a nasty piece of work by all accounts. This King Crow is calling all the crows to a great gathering, the reason for which is still unknown, but from what we've experienced in the last few days, it's bound to be something pretty awful. That crow you bonked on the head yesterday, Anna, was one of his sons. They weren't expecting any courageous actions and I think that they may be laying low licking their wounds. However, we can be sure that they won't forget your little band now, and are probably planning something nasty at this very moment. What did you find out, Sidney?"

"Well, I kept the barn patrol in sight all morning, and you were going at a pretty good rate considering how hot the sun was, you suddenly disappeared under a large willow tree, and so I came down to see you. When I landed, I found you all safe and comfortably asleep in its shadow, and very lovely it felt too, after flying in that blazing sun. I decided to leave you there and fly over to Wood-on-the-Hill. I was halfway there when some rabbits flagged me down on a low hilltop. They told me that a terrible new King Crow had sent word for all the foxes, stoats and weasels in the surrounding countryside to come to a meeting tomorrow morning at Wood-on-the-Hill. They also said that they couldn't understand how a crow had such power to be able to order the animals about like that. They'd never known it before. Not since during the reign of old Baron Buck Rabbit, as the legend goes. There's got to be something bigger behind this, they say."

"Anyway, a hare runner was sent to Badger's Wood and there's a meeting up there at sundown tonight. They know all about the barn patrol and told me that it would be a good idea if either Sam or I were there at that meeting."

"Right, I'll go," said Sam, immediately. "Sidney, you fly up home and do the Holly and Poppy run, then come back and remain with the patrol until I return." When I awoke the following morning, Sam and Sidney were having a serious talk down at the edge of the lake. I wandered down and asked what the plan for today was.

Sam turned to me with a serious look on his face. "The plan for today is, to get you and the patrol as far away from here as possible and finally back to the safety of your homes."

"Why?" I replied, "What did you find out at Badgers Wood last night and what about our expedition to the river?"

"Things are much more serious than we thought," said Sam. "I must talk to you alone, Anna. I'm afraid that you will not reach the river on this trip."

He turned back to Sidney. "Get everybody up and ready to move in one hour, have a quick breakfast with the leftovers from yesterday. I'm going to take Anna to the top of that next hill and explain to her what is happening and what we must do."

"Right," said Sidney. "See you back here within the hour."

Chapter 12
Wood-On-The-Hill

"Hold tight!" said Sam and picking me up in his long beak, he leapt into the air. After a few wobbly flaps of his wings, we rose into the sky, the grass, trees and bushes getting smaller and smaller as we climbed higher. The view was amazing, I could see for miles, I looked back and saw the village and Badgers Wood, and farther away in the distance Wood-on-the-Hill, the black cloud of crows buzzing once more about its treetops. I then looked in the direction which we were flying. Immediately in front of us was a bare hilltop covered with grass and Sam was heading straight for it. In the valley beyond this hill, I saw a wide band of water which stretched across from left to right of our middle distance, beyond that everything became hazy in the morning mist.

"The Big River," I said in wonder, as we came to land on the top of the hill.

"That's about as close as you'll get this trip," said Sam, as he placed me gently on the grass.

"Oh dear," I replied. "Things sound pretty bad; I hope we're not in too much of a mess."

"I'm afraid we are," said the large bird, "and we must hurry. The story I heard at Badgers Wood last night is almost unbelievable and very frightening.

I sat and listened as Sam told me what he had heard. "This King Crow, although pretty terrible is small fry compared to the real bad guy. His name is Ubitz, and he and his followers are strange and ugly creatures called Dooms. They dwell deep down in the lower tunnels near the earth's centre warmth; they are a tough breed, last heard of only in legend. He has come up with some of his followers, from his tunnel kingdom below and such is his power, he has taken over command of the crows. He has called a meeting of all the bad guys this morning over at Wood-on-the-Hill."

"But why has all this suddenly happened?" I asked in amazement.

"It seems that nobody knows," he replied, "But over at Badger's Wood I heard a rumour whispered about, that the Barn Patrol have more than a trip to the big river in mind and that's what brought this evil lot up from down below.

"Bill Badger's holding something back, I don't know what it is yet, but we'll get to the bottom of it in the end. For now, he's willing to help Sidney and me to get you away from here as soon as possible."

"But it was only a trip to the Big River!" I said, in total disbelief of the story that I had just heard.

"I know," said Sam, "But as I said before, the badgers and rabbits know more than they're telling.

Come on, let's go back down to the others and get you all out of here."

I took one last look at the river, to try to remember the picture for our book, and then I was whisked up into the sky again in Sam's big beak.

We hadn't been in the air for a few minutes, when we saw Sidney flying towards us at a great speed.

Soon he was flying along the side of us. "Terrible news!" he shouted. "Some stoats and foxes have kidnapped Polly and headed off with her towards Wood-on-the Hill."

"What!" shouted Sam, and suddenly I had the feeling that I was falling through the air, which I was. When Sam had shouted out "what!" he had forgotten all about me and I had toppled from his beak and was falling rapidly towards the ground.

Luckily, Sidney had spotted what had happened, and, diving down, scooped me out of the sky beneath. He brought me down to a field and Sam came flapping down beside us. "Sorry about that, Anna," he said, and turning to Sidney, asked him to tell us what had happened.

Polly, Lindy and the rats had gone off to gather some nuts and mushrooms and things for the trip home. Polly had strayed off on her own, and it seemed by the signs and tracks, that she had been taken by a band of stoats and foxes and their trail headed off in the direction of Wood-on-the-Hill."

"I couldn't stop the others, they went off in chase," said Sidney, quite upset.

"Goodness gracious, what is happening and why?" exclaimed Sam in anger.

"Now Sidney, you try to locate Lindy and the others. When you find them, tell them not to confront the stoats and foxes if they catch up with them, just stay on their track. I'll take Anna and fly over to alert badger and the others, we may, with luck, see Polly and her kidnappers on the way. If so, we can direct badger and his boys to cut them off between Badgers Wood and Wood-on-the-Hill. Whatever happens we'll meet back at Badgers Wood this afternoon.

My heart was thumping with worry as Sam picked me up and we set off back in the direction we had come earlier that morning. Sidney went off in a direct line towards Wood-on-the-Hill.

On arriving at the campsite, we could see the tracks in the long grass heading off into the distance, looking further on we could see Sidney circle round and round in the air and disappear down behind some trees, he had obviously found the rest of the barn patrol.

"Right," said Sam, "I think we'll head straight for Badgers Wood, grab your bag and we'll be off.

We rose high into the air, Sam's huge wings carried us along at a great pace, my eyes watered and blurred my vision, but I thought that I saw our little patrol and Sidney way beneath me and then going on from them another set of tracks disappearing off to our right. When we arrived at Badgers Wood, it was late morning, and we could see from above that Bill Badger had called together all the good animals for a meeting. There was a huge crowd of animals gathered round a large tree stump in a clearing in the middle of the wood, and on it stood a large badger, that must be Bill, I thought. As we descended all the animals looked upwards, I could see rabbits, badgers, squirrels, voles, mice, otters and many others. We landed on the edge of the clearing and the animals parted as we made our way to the centre tree stump.

Sam climbed up onto the stump and I scrambled up behind him. "I'm afraid that things have moved along faster than we thought," gasped Sam between breaths. "A band of stoats and foxes have taken Polly, one of the kittens, and headed off towards Wood-on-the-Hill."

I heard a few tut…tuts and murmurings coming from the animals together with a lot of head nodding.

"We know," said the large badger. "We picked up a couple of weasels spying on us from the edge of the wood, they told us about the kidnappers. I've sent our best otter patrol to lie in wait for them in the tall grass meadows this side of Wood-on-the-Hill.

"We are now having a meeting to try and get to the bottom of this mystery."

"Okay," replied Sam. "Can I leave Anna with you whilst I head off to try and find the rest of our patrol?" Bill Badger nodded his head slowly. I could tell that he wasn't very pleased with us and that went for the other animals too.

I wanted to go with Sam to search for Polly and was about to say so but one look at Bill Badger and I realised that the decisions were now being made by wiser heads than mine, so I sat on the tree stump at the badger's feet feeling small, slightly unwanted and very worried about my dear sister Polly. Sam finally rose into the air and flew away over the tops of the trees. The big badger stooped down and gave me a couple of gentle pats on the head with his huge paw. The animal's meeting continued on around me. There was lots of talk about Legends, magic seeds Ubitz, the Dooms, crows and bad guys but everybody talked so fast and some in the strangest accents that I couldn't make much out. I was also very tired after my flying experience and soon dropped off to sleep.

When I woke up, I found myself laying in a comfortable bed of the softest moss and leaves in the glow of a cosy fire. I thought that I was dreaming, but after rubbing my eyes a few times the fire was still there. I looked around the cosy little room; there was a blue door on one side and a green door on the other. What must have woken me was the babble of voices coming from the other side of the green door. The voices got louder and louder until finally the door burst open and in tumbled the rest of my patrol, followed, to my relief, by Polly and Bill Badger. What a joy I felt seeing Polly there with my friends. I rubbed my eyes again in disbelief but happily it was all real.

"Ah, you've finally woken up," said Bill Badger. "I thought that you'd taken up hibernating, you've slept so long."

Everybody then started asking questions at the same time until Bill shouted over the top of us all, "Hold on, Hold on, we'll have plenty of time for talk and explanations later but now I think that you should all eat," and as he said this, he pushed the blue door open and led us into a large room with a long table spread with delicious food and lit by another cosy log fire at the far end.

The old badger sat us all down and told us to tuck in. There were names at each chair, and I sat down next to Polly and gave her a little hug, "You and your adventurous ways," I said. "We nearly lost you that time."

"Oh, it wasn't that bad, the foxes were a bit aloof, but the stoats were pretty chatty. Apparently, they had been told to look out for cats, rats and a lamb, so they grabbed me in passing," she said casually.

"No, seriously, Polly, I was so worried I didn't know what to do. I don't think I'll ever go trekking again, that's if we ever get home."

"Humbug and poppycock," said Polly. "Of course you will get home and of course you'll go trekking again, it's in your blood now. Anyway, you seem to have forgotten that I had Patch's Swordstick with me given solely for my protection."

"You don't mean to say that you used it?" I said in alarm.

"I didn't have to, I just had to touch its handle in my belt, and everybody took three steps back, none of them are very brave you know."

"Well, it's still lucky that the otters rescued you," I replied. "From what I've heard so far, of this Baron Ubitz, your luck would have run out if they'd have got you to Wood-on-the-Hill."

We tucked into the splendid food, until finally Bill Badger gave a couple of low coughs to gain our attention. He was standing at the end of the table with his back to the fire smoking a long clay pipe.

"Now then," he said in a gruff voice to us all in general, "What do you think you're up to? You've certainly upset the whole of the countryside between Swan Lake and the big river, especially that lot over at Wood-on-the-Hill."

The others all turned and looked in my direction. Here goes, I thought and stood up, "First of all, Mr

Badger, may I thank you for bringing my sister back safely to us."

"Yes! Yes! Yes!" he replied, impatiently. "That's quite all right, but what the devil are you up to?"

"Well, we just wanted to see where our spinney stream met the big river, and Sam and Sidney stork agreed to help us with our expedition."

"What! Is that it?" spluttered the badger. "No Magic Seeds?"

"What Magic Seeds?" We all asked in one voice.

"We'll get onto that in a minute," he said gruffly.

"What's all the trouble over at Wood-on-the-Hill?" butted in Polly in her usual cheeky way. "The stoats told me that they had been called to a meeting and to look out for our patrol on the way."

"What else did they tell you?" went on Bill. "Think hard Polly it may be important."

"They said that they had travelled from the Land of Lower Big River and that the foxes had force, marched their band night and day. Oh, and that the crows had flown down to tell them about the meeting."

"Ah, that is why they were so easy to ambush in the long meadows, they must have been very tired. Did you hear anything else?"

"I overheard two foxes muttering something about some chaps named Ubitz and King Crow, but I couldn't make it out, they shut up when they saw that I was close by."

"Ah, ah!" exclaimed Bill Badger. "King Crow again then, there is something afoot. But I think that King Crow and his master Baron Ubitz have got the wrong end of the stick. You see, from information that we have gathered, the crows have been reporting back, that, as you headed south, each day you sent out a team who gathered all the nuts, seeds and berries and carried them back to your camp for inspection."

"We did," cut in Lindy, "But they were to eat."

"That's what I mean by the wrong end of the stick," said Bill. "They think that you are an expedition searching for the magic seeds."

"What Magic Seeds?" we all repeated in one voice.

"Well, most of it is legend," went on the badger, and the rest are stories which have been passed down from generation to generation. The Legend of old is this; in days long ago there lived a King and Queen otter. They ruled over all the lands which lay between Swan Lake to the north, and Lower Big River to the south, and the same distance to the east and west. They were happy times, and the King and Queen were blessed with a son, a prince, and when this prince reached the age of twenty-one, they gave a big birthday party. Many wisemen, wizards and witches were invited to the prince's party, and they travelled from far and wide to pay their respects to this honourable family.

The Legend says that one of these wisemen brought a present of twenty-one seeds for the boy, and on the day of the birthday, the King scattered these seeds on the top of a hill which stood close to the castle. The following day, there were twenty-one beautiful fully-grown oak trees on top of the hill. They called them, The Twenty-One Trees or The Princes Crown.

The wiseman also stated that, as long as there was a tree left growing on the hill, peace would reign over the world.

In time, the Twenty-One Trees expanded right over the hill, and it is known today as Wood-on-the-Hill. In the centre of the wood there still remains one big old oak, this is the last remaining descendant of the original twenty-one.

It is said, that each year this tree still produces the Magic Seeds, or miniature acorns as we know them. Beneath the tree is a labyrinth of tunnels, and according to the stories of old, each year the crop of golden acorns are taken down these tunnels and stored in large caves, deep in the bowels of the earth.

The original Keepers of the Seeds were elected from the wisest men in the kingdom, they were good people and were treated like holy men. They decided that by storing the Seeds safely underground that they would insure peace on earth forever.

However, as time went by and each generation of wise men guarded the seeds, they became more and more possessive about them, and now we have Baron Ubitz, the ruler of the lower kingdoms; he is the worst yet. A hoarder, who is deeply suspicious of anyone who shows the slightest interest in his store of Golden Acorns.

"Wow! And is all this true?" said Roy to the badger. "If legends come true, it may well be," replied Bill, "And this Baron Ubitz seems to have a strange power over the nasty guys. I think that the best thing to do is to pack you all off back home, and send a message over to Wood-on-the-Hill explaining that you weren't doing what they thought you were doing. Whether they believe us or not will have to be seen, in the meantime, I think you should all get a good night's sleep. I've arranged with your stork friends for them to come back early in the morning and take you back home. He led us through the blue door and out through the green door, up a long passage to a room with beds all along one wall. "This is where our guests sleep, and might I suggest you put your heads down very soon, you've got some hard trekking to do tomorrow.

We awoke the next morning and were quickly escorted through the badger's tunnels and up into the brilliant sunlight of the clearing. Here, we found Sam and Sidney in deep conversation with Bill Badger, and as we arrived they turned to greet us.

"Good morning, Barn Patrol," said Sam with a smile.

"Well, it seems that the best thing we can do is to get you as far away from here as possible and hope that things here will then calm back down for Bill and his friends."

"Okay," I said, and turning to Bill Badger, I thanked him for all his help and hospitality and apologised for the upset that we had caused to him and his friends. He put his large forearm around my shoulder and walked me over to the edge of the clearing.

"Anna," he said in his gruff old voice, "You did not cause all the upset. The danger has always been lurking there under Wood-on-the-Hill, we chose to ignore it, and your innocent little expedition just happened to trigger off something underground. I can tell you now that the Legend is a reality, in fact I actually have one of the Golden Acorns." He then produced from his waistcoat pocket a small wooden box, and secretly opened it in such a way that nobody else could see what he was doing. Inside was a beautiful tiny golden acorn. He snapped the box shut and pressed it into my paw.

"This is one of a pair, they were brought out from the caves some time ago by a very brave little mole named Morris. In order to test the truth of the Legend; one day, last year, Morris and I took the other acorn and planted it, next to the stream, some miles north of the village. When we awoke the next day, a beautiful fully-grown willow tree was standing on the very spot.

I gasped in surprise, "I have seen this tree! We all slept beneath it yesterday, it has wonderful healing powers, we were exhausted and only dozed for an hour, but upon awakening we felt totally refreshed and marched for a further five hours without food or drink."

The old badger smiled knowingly and continued, "Unfortunately, Morris went back underground for some more seeds. This was six weeks ago, and we have heard nothing from him since then. So, you see, you cannot blame yourselves, it could have been Morris that upset the Dooms."

"But what shall I do with the Golden Acorn," I whispered urgently.

"The Legend goes on to say, that wherever in the world a Golden Acorn is planted, the tree that grows shall take on the appearance and characteristics of the surrounding trees of that country. This has been partly proven by our willow tree, but for definite proof an acorn should be planted in a foreign land."

"But why is it so important?" I asked.

"It is said by some very wise humans that the world will slowly die if we lose all the rain forests. Shall I explain any further?"

"No," I replied. "I think I understand," and I suddenly thought of Poppy, Holly, Mum and Dad, and

Dad saying that one day soon he would take them on holiday to the island of Barbados.

"I think I have the answer," I said, as I slipped the little box into my bag.

"I thought you might," he growled quietly. "Not a word to anyone."

We both turned and strolled slowly back to join the others, my mind was turned upside down from what Bill Badger had just told me.

"Ready?" I said, a little shakily.

"Yes," came the firm reply from the patrol and after saying our goodbyes to Bill Badger and his friends, we left the clearing, our bags bulging with food for the journey.

Sam and Sidney flew off to see if the bad guys were up to anything. They had been quiet ever since Polly's rescue; however they must have had their meeting by now and what decisions they had made we could only guess at. Our guess was that they had Badger's Wood surrounded and that we would all be taken prisoner any minute. Bill Badger had sent two hare patrols out before we left. One patrol took the peace message to Wood-on-the-Hill, the other was to do a swift circuit of Badger's Wood and check that the coast was clear for our get-away.

No sooner had we entered the wood than we began to hear all sorts of suspicious noises. We were all a bit scared you see, and the least thing made us jump. We heard a loud noise up ahead of us and all dived for cover in some thick shrub. To our relief three hares came jogging along the track and we scrambled out to meet them.

"There's nobody around outside the wood for at least two fields," said the leader. "But we did pick up these suspicious looking characters on the way in," and three more hares came up the track escorting Patchy, Marmite and Wellington between them. Patchy ran up to Polly and gave her a big hug.

"It's okay," I said to the hares. "They're friends of ours and jolly good it is to see them too. They will help us to get to the other side of the village."

We thanked the hares for the information and for finding our friends and they headed out to the fringe of the wood.

As we crept out from the cover of the undergrowth which skirted the wood, Rob, who was leading, exclaimed, "Oh no!" and we all froze in our tracks.

"What is it?" I hissed, and looking out we could see that the sky over towards Wood-on-the-Hill was full of crows, rooks and magpies wheeling slowly in circles and gradually working their way towards us.

"What shall we do now?"

"What shall we do now?" said Walt and Will nervously, and everybody turned to me for an answer.

"If we make a dash for it, they'll pick us up easily, so let's just lay low here and see what they do." I said not really knowing what to do. The birds continued their slow searching pattern getting closer and closer to us as we lay dead still in the undergrowth. I wondered where the two storks could be. Sam would have an answer if he were here.

Then the black mass of birds were directly overhead, I thought that we would be spotted at any minute and closed my eyes and wished and wished that they would go away. My wish sort of came true, because when I opened my eyes again, I noticed that the main body of birds had drifted on towards the village and the sky above us was slowly clearing. We all kept perfectly still until there were no more birds overhead and I whispered quietly, "Right, we'll give it fifteen minutes then we'll head off."

Then Marmite suddenly said, "We know a secret way under the hedgerows that leads all the way back to the village!"

"But that's our own secret path!" piped up Wellington. "We said that we'd never ever tell anyone about that, not even Ginger or Mimsy."

"Hey! Come on now you two, now's not the time for all that, these chaps need all the help they can get by the looks of it," butted in Patch, theatrically. "It's like the French underground movement, in fact we can be the Kitten underground movement. Come on! And he disappeared into a little tunnel in the hedgerow leading along the tree line away from the wood. We all followed at a brisk pace. Most of the time we could just about walk upright, but sometimes Lindy and us kittens had to crawl along on our bellies; it was alright for the rats they were that much smaller. We made good progress and every now and then Marmite, Wellington or Patch would sneak a look to see where we were.

We were getting close to the village when Patch returned after one of these reconnoitres. "I can see the church tower and some of the roof tops, and guess what? They are black with birds, so thick that you can't even see the roofs for them, and they're just sitting there quietly waiting...it's right eerie—like that movie—what's it called now."

"Oh, shut up, Patchy," said Marmite, impatiently, "How are we going to get through to Mimsy and Ginger?"

"Why do we have to get through to Mimsy and Ginger?" asked Lindy. "Why don't we just skirt around the village?"

"Because our tunnel leads right to home and there's another one that we can take straight out the other side of the village," said Patch. Besides, we'd never live it down if we didn't take you back to see Mimsy, she's not stopped talking about you guys since you left the other day. Swears she should have gone with you, relatives by the river and all that; never leaves her cushion but means well you know. No, we always have to report in to Mimsy—she'll have a plan."

"Right now, I've got a plan," said Marmite. "Why don't Wellington and I go down on the village green and create a diversion. We can mock-up a catfight and make a real hullabaloo. That should distract the birds long enough for you to disappear into the house unnoticed."

"I say, that's pretty brave of you," I said.

Wellington added, "Oh, don't mention it. Marmite always comes up with good ideas."

I could tell by her tone of voice that she wasn't too keen on the idea.

"Jolly good, you two," said Patch, taking over command of the situation. "If the birds get too restless and become outright dangerous, make a run for home, and watch out for that Mrs Cribble in Rose Cottage. She'll have a bucket of water over you the minute you start making a row. Now, off you go, we'll creep further along the passage and run when we hear you start up."

We crawled further along under the bushes. Patch popped his head out from under a privet hedge just as Wellington and Marmite started their din. He darted back in, "Quick!" he said, "All the birds are watching those two capering about, it's like the first night at the proms—follow me."

We scurried along after him, out of the bushes by the kitchen door and shot into the house.

"Well done," I said, as Will, the last one in skidded round the kitchen door to safety. "I hope that Wellington and Marmite are O K," We could still hear their row, in fact, it seemed as if it was getting louder, and mixed in with it was the sound of a human voice.

Patch sneaked a look out of the kitchen window, "The show has still got the audience's undivided attention," he said. "Just look at them."

I looked out of the window and, sure enough, I saw the backs of rows and rows of crows, rooks and magpies as they jockeyed for a better view of the scrap. The sounds came to a climax and then what sounded like a large splash and then silence. A murmuring was heard from the rooftops, and all went quiet again. Patch took us along the hallway and ushered us through the door of the lounge, there on her cushion sat Mimsy, quite awake.

"Hallo, my little band of travellers," she purred, "Lovely to see you again so soon. How's the river? Did you get to the palace? But you must have flown darlings. Tut! Patchy. What was that din? Has somebody robbed the post office? And all these birds, the domestics really shouldn't put so much out on the bird table. Oh, and where's Marmite and Wellington?" At that moment there was a scurrying sound outside the door and in came the other two kittens. A dry, smug Marmite and a soggy looking Wellington.

"What have you been up to?" said Mimsy in alarm.

"Upsetting that nice Mrs Cribble again by the looks of things, Wellington, go and get cleaned up immediately: it's nearly lunch time."

"Talking of lunch time," I said, "Allow us to repay your hospitality with a splendid meal courtesy of Bill Badger," and I proceeded to lay the food out from my bag. The others followed my lead until we had a grand spread covering the lounge floor.

"Old Bill Badger," purred Mimsy. "Is he still living up there in the wood? The dear old thing, he's been there forever. My, my, my no wonder, he certainly eats well," she continued looking at the food laid out in front of her.

At that moment, who should conveniently pop his head round the door but Ginger.

"Mmmm, just in time for lunch. Oh! Sorry, Mimsy didn't realise you had guests."

"Hallo Ginger, what a surprise to see you. Don't go, stay and have a bite," she said, with the sweetest of smiles.

"Oh, I say old girl, that's awfully good of you. Hallo to you all. Did you have a successful journey?" he said, turning to us with a mouthful of raspberry sandwich. You know, I was having a quiet snooze under the lavender, when all of a sudden there was this almighty din which woke me up; sounded like a right catfight. Anyway, I looked up and there were birds everywhere, all over the roofs, not the thing really, you know."

"Yes, alright, Ginger," went on Mimsy. "Let's just settle down and enjoy lunch, shall we?"

And so, we did, joined by a much drier Wellington, we all munched away until most of the food had disappeared.

Ginger ambled off out of the door, Mimsy dropped off to sleep, and we told our adventure quietly to the three kittens, using Rob and Roy's sketches to remind us.

"Crickey!" said Patch, "You lot don't muck about do you? I wish I had come, I don't know about that lot up there though," he said, raising his eyes towards the ceiling. "They're not a very happy bunch, are they?"

"Who's that?" said Mimsy, waking up. "If anybody isn't happy it's their own fault, we have two choices in this world, we can either be happy or we can be sad, so that's that; now Patchy, let's sort out some sleeping arrangements for our guests."

"If it's all the same to you, ma'am, thank you very much, but I think we ought to press on." I said with the slightest hint of a bow.

"I don't know, you youngsters, always in a hurry, no time to stop and think, let alone talk. If you must then you must. Where will you sleep tonight?"

"We're hoping to make the dam before nightfall, we camped there on the way down," I replied.

"That's a long way," purred the large white cat, "You should stay here tonight, then you'll have a whole day tomorrow to get to the dam."

I knew that she was right, but something inside me said that we must press on. I was also worried about Sam and Sidney and wanted to get out to some clear sky to see if there was any sign of the two storks, but then, of course, there was the ever-watchful flock of nasty birds. Oh dear, I thought to myself, I have got my chums into a bit of a mess.

"No!" I said firmly. "Thank you for the invite Mimsy, but we've arranged to meet Sam stork up by the dam, and he'll worry if we're not there."

"Then, go you must," she replied. "But next time you're passing, you must stay longer. We've got plenty of room especially when the humans go away."

I thanked her again, said my goodbye and followed the others out into the hallway.

Patch turned to us, "It's going to be a bit easier going out," he said, and led us down a steep flight of steps. We walked between tall racks of wine bottles through what must have been the cellar. At the end, he climbed stealthily up a vertical metal ladder, secured into the wall, at the top he stopped, put his finger to his lips and gently pushed upwards against the roof. A dim light suddenly lit us up and we all clambered through the trap door into a hedgerow tunnel very much like the one that we had come in by."

"Hey cool," said Lindy. "You guys seem to have this village well planned out."

"Yes, we do take a certain pride in our achievements," said Patch, proudly. "Anyway, enough of that. Now, this tunnel will take us well clear of the village to its north, and we'll leave those silly birds sitting pretty—Come on!"

We followed after Patch, with Marmite and Wellington bringing up the rear. After about twenty minutes, Patch stopped, "This is where we must leave you," he said. "Just out there is your stream, although it's pretty dried up now. You've still got what's left of your food, and whilst you were saying goodbye to Mimsy, back at the house, we filled all your water bottles; so, with a bit of luck you may make the dam before dark."

He then turned and gave Polly his usual hug. We all said our goodbyes and promised to come back and see them as soon as we could. The three of them then crept out to see if the coast was clear.

"Okay," whispered Patch, and we all clambered out from the hedgerow onto the bank of our old spinney stream. Looking back, we saw the black mass of the birds covering the distant village. I noticed that one or two of them were getting a little restless fluttering high into the sky, wheeling around and then dropping back down to join the rest.

"Come on, Patrol," I said quietly. "Goodbye Patch, goodbye Marmite, goodbye Wellington. Thanks for everything. See you soon," and off we set northwards along the bank of the stream.

"Wait!" said Polly, and she ran back to where Patch was standing. I saw her try to give him back his sword-stick, which she had carried in her belt ever since he had given it to her. "No," I heard him say to her, "You may need it yet, it's yours forever now." They gave a last hug and Polly raced after us. As she passed by me, I saw the sun twinkle in a little tear in the corner of her eye.

We had been travelling well for about three hours, the sun was dropping fast towards the trees to our west, and I realised that we were not going to make the dam for our night's camp. We had slowed down because the crow patrols were about again, they must have realised by now, back at the village, that we had managed to slip through.

Chapter 13
Surrounded

It was getting pretty late now, and I still hadn't decided about where to camp. Our only option was to huddle down in the dry stream bed for the night.

I was about to tell the others to start looking for a likely spot, when three crows, flying low over the grass, spotted us out in the open.

The leading bird gave out a loud squawk of delight and his two mates soon joined in the chorus.

We all stopped in our tracks, "That's the last thing we need," said Lindy. "We'll never make the dam tonight and now this."

"Yes," I said, completely lost for an answer. "I was thinking that we could camp in the stream bed, if we could find a nice overhanging bank or something, but now this puts a different light on it.'

The three crows had settled in a nearby tree and were cawing away to each other.

"I hope they don't send back for their friends," I said, giving them a sidelong glance.

"Look!" I continued, "I've had an idea; if we split up into three groups, each bird will have to follow a separate group leaving none to send back to bring the others."

"Brill!" cried the rats together.

"Okay then," I said, "Polly, you take Rob and head west towards the sun; Lindy and Roy go east and Walt and Will you come with me, we'll take the stream bed."

"We'll all make our own routes and then swing back in to meet up at the dam tomorrow about lunchtime. We wait there until we're all together again. If anybody fails to turn up, then the remaining patrol members must send out search parties until they are found. Good luck everyone, let's go!"

"Oh no, look!" cried Polly, and we all spun round in the direction which she was pointing.

Our hopes were dashed for one of the crows had left the others and was flying back in the direction of the village.

"We've got to stay together now and travel as fast as we can along the direction we were heading in, and hope that we can find some sort of cover for the night. I don't know what those birds are planning, but if they try to attack us, we'd better have our staves at the ready."

Then I had a brainwave.

"The Willow Tree!" I exclaimed.

"That crow is certain to come back with the whole flock and if we can make it to the Magic Willow Tree, it may just protect us from them."

"How far is it?" asked Walt.

"I can't remember for sure. It's about three hours since we left Patch and the others. It can't be that far away."

The stream wound from side to side across the Lowlands in big snaking loops, so I decided that we would take a more direct route, only touching the stream each time it looped back in our direction.

The going was more difficult as it meant pushing through waste-high grass, but it would be quicker than following the stream. I looked ahead into the distance and could just make out the first tree in a line of willows. That's got to be them I thought to myself.

"I can see the willows," I shouted back to the others, "They must be about three miles away."

At that moment, one of the crows circling high above us, gave a mighty squawk and looking back towards the village I could make out a low grey cloud.

"Keep going," I urged the others and turning around I waved my stave furiously in the air.

Now, there were about fifty birds wheeling about above us and many more joining them by the second. They didn't seem to have much idea about formation flying and were spending most of the time trying to avoid one another, nevertheless, some were managing to swoop down on the patrol and the staves were flying.

Polly and Lindy made it to the first willow, which gave them some protection, but the little rats were slower. I did my best to keep them going, we were all near exhaustion and I saw Will and Walt stumble a few times.

Suddenly, in front of my eyes, poor old Walt was plucked off the ground by his knapsack and disappeared into the black mass above.

There was nothing I could do as Rob, Roy and Wilt all disappeared in front of my eyes. I was obviously too heavy but had a nasty time fighting my way to the Big Willow Tree. I stumbled under its welcoming branches and lay there gasping for air.

"They've taken the rats," I choked in despair.

"Oh dear, I wish we had never set out on this silly adventure," spluttered Lindy through her tears. "What are we going to do now, our poor dear rats."

As we looked out from under the hanging willow branches, we could see the crows landing all around us until we were totally surrounded by a sea of black bobbing heads.

"I wonder what they've done with Rob, Roy, Walt and Will," whispered Polly also in tears.

I spotted a much larger crow with an extra circle of feathers on his head, standing apart from the main crowd with a group of larger birds.

"Look, that must be King Crow," I said to the others.

"Yes, and they must be his brothers with him," went on Lindy. "One's got a plaster on his head where you bonked him the other day."

They certainly looked pretty ferocious strutting about, but I think that I was right about the Willow, they all seemed very wary of it.

Sure enough, the Willow's magic was somehow affecting the birds and it was also giving us extra hope. I could feel my strength returning and I'm certain that the Willow then gave me my second brainwave of the day.

"Listen," I said to the others, "Suppose we coax old King Crow under the tree with a tasty tit-bit, it might have a nice friendly effect on him, has anybody got any food left?"

The three of us looked from one to the other and finally Polly said, rather guiltily, "Well, back at Mimsy's, I had a poke around in the kitchen whilst you were talking. I knew that we had to make the dam tonight, so

I borrowed these for our supper," and she emptied onto the grass the contents of her bag.

"Polly, you whizz! What luck," I shouted, patting her on the back, and picking up a nice piece of fruitcake with lovely big nuts sticking out of it.

"This will do very nicely for a big hungry crow."

Meanwhile, the crows had jostled the four rats out in front of them and we were all relieved to see that they seemed alright.

"Are you okay?" I shouted out to them.

"Yes," came back a nervous reply from Rob. "I don't think I'll ever take to flying though."

I then walked slowly towards the edge of the tree and placed the piece of cake a short distance under the tree's shadow then walked back to join the others.

The crows started cawing quietly and picking up the smell of the delicious piece of cake, King Crow and his buddies waddled a bit closer. They must have been pretty hungry after the long flight and sure enough after a bit more cawing, two of the larger birds sidled under the shadow of the Willow Tree towards the cake.

As soon as they were under the tree, the strangest thing happened. They hooked their wings together and started to dance a jig around and round the cake.

"It's working," I whispered to Polly and Lindy, as I saw King Crow cock his head to one side and give a long low caw.

The other two crows stopped their jig, took a little nibble each and continued their dance. This was finally too much for King Crow who hopped under the tree to join them. He, in turn, started his own little dance and having had a taste of the cake turned back to the group of larger crows and gave another long low caw.

Rob, Roy, Walt and Will were then nudged gently towards the tree by many large ugly black beaks. They quickly got the idea and scurried over to join us looking extremely relieved.

Polly and I then took the rest of the food and laid it in a circle around the edge of the tree and we all stood next to the Willow's trunk to watch what happened next.

King Crow, followed by his brothers and then by the whole flock of birds danced their strange jig right round under the furthest branches of the big old willow tree, each bird taking one peck of food on the way and then hopping and jigging one behind the other finally flying off in a line in the direction of the distant village, and as the last bird took to the air I turned to my friends, "Whew," I said. "That was very scary indeed, I think we'll stay here tonight. Anybody hungry?"

"No!" Came the chorus back and we all did our own little dance round the tree trunk. Looking up, we saw the hanging branches of the Willow Tree swaying in time to our dance. We all laughed in joyful relief and then settled down to a well-deserved sleep under the protective cover of the Big Old Willow.

The next thing I knew, I was being gently nudged awake by a long beak. I awoke with a scare, thinking that the crows had returned, but, looked up into the friendly face of Sam Stork.

"Boy, am I glad to see you," I said.

Chapter 14

Home at Last

It was still an hour before dark, so we sat in a circle around the two storks and told them our story.

"You're certainly right about this tree," said Sidney. "I feel as if I could fly twice round the world and back again."

"Yes," I replied. "It really changed those crows into nice guys. What a stroke of luck it was to remember that old Willow Tree."

"I don't think we'll ever forget it now," chimed in Polly.

"So, what have you been doing today?" I said, joking to Sam.

"We flew over to Wood-on-the-Hill, the hares had delivered Bill Badger's message by then and we were summoned to see King Crow."

At the village, they all believed the story about the Barn-patrol, so the crow said, but the Baron also wanted to know if the Patrol knew anything about the Magic Seeds. What Magic Seeds! I exclaimed, and this seemed to pacify the big crow. He obviously thought that if I knew nothing about the Seeds, then you most certainly didn't.

Anyway, he went off into the forest to talk to Ubitz again and on his return said that he had orders to send Sidney and I back to Badger's Wood with some of his crows and stay there until the rest of his gang had seen the Barn Patrol off their land. So that's where we had to stay and very worrying it was too. They must have frightened you with their bullying and thanks to this wonderful tree you are all safe now."

"Did you see King Crow again?" I asked.

"Yes," replied Sidney. "To our surprise, about two hours ago, a long line of crows flew towards Badger's Wood with King Crow leading them, they circled over the wood, cawing peacefully. Then our escort flew up and joined them and they all went off in a line towards Wood-on-the-Hill. Bill Badger and the others were very pleased about it, so we said our goodbyes and came to find you. Now, I think we've had enough excitement for one day, we'll sleep here tonight and head for home in the morning."

"There's another cloud!" shouted Lindy in alarm pointing towards the village, and we all looked anxiously in that direction, expecting to see the crows returning.

Sure enough, hanging over the horizon was a menacing black cloud. "That one is real weather," she said with a mischievous grin, and we all laughed at her naughtiness.

We all woke up in the morning to the wonderful sound of bubbling water. Lindy's weather cloud, from the night before, had brought the first of the autumn rains and our spinney stream was singing merrily away beside us. The large friendly willow had acted as a giant umbrella and kept us dry all through the storm.

"The storm was fantastic," said Sam. "With lots of beautiful lightning flashes, but you all slept right through it, you must have been very tired."

Head for home, I think that was the phrase that Sam used and that is most certainly what we did. After a breakfast of mushrooms and nuts, washed down with ice-cool stream water, we said goodbye to the wonderful Willow Tree and set off north towards the dam, Swan Lake and everything that meant home to us.

We reached the dam about mid-day. It was good to be back in familiar surroundings, we even laughed joyfully when Percy Pike took two big leaps into the air. The water rats said that it was his way of saying welcome home, but Rob thought that it was the fishes' way of saying, "Here comes dinner again."

We camped, that night, by the bridge under which our stream flowed before emptying into the lake. It hadn't rained during the day, but I instructed everyone to build a bivouac from dried branches and leaves, and it was just as well that we did, because that night, it poured down again. We all sat in the entrances of our little shelters and watched the amazing show of thunder and lightning.

The following morning, we slept late and awoke to a crisp autumn day, as we walked past the farm all seemed quiet and peaceful.

"Look," said Polly, making us all jump, and she pointed up into the sky. Three crows were flapping lazily across the sky, cawing to each other in a friendly manner.

"Do you think they're looking for us?" she said, cheekily.

"Polly," I said, "Won't you ever be serious about anything?"

"No," she replied, and everybody laughed.

We finally reached the spinney.

Walt and Will dived straight into the water. "This will be our new home," they cried, "And you can all come and see us every day."

Polly, Lindy and I crawled through the hole in the hedgerow and there across the backfield was our beloved barn and next to it, Home.

It was so good to see, and I felt a tear of joy trickle down my cheek.

Sam and Sidney were slowly circling above the roofs and in the window of the top room, I could just make out two little figures waving frantically in our direction. Holly and Poppy, what an adventure we had to tell them.

We all raced each other across the field; Rob and Roy disappeared into the barn, Lindy had met her Aunt Lucinda and was strolling off to see her mum, Polly and I scrambled through the hole in the fence and bumped straight into two pairs of children's shoes and we looked up into two happy smiling faces. Holly and Poppy scooped us off the ground and showered us with hugs and kisses.

"You're half a day early," said Poppy, "I've been ticking it off on my calendar."

The girls took off our backpacks, hid them under a flowerpot and carried us into the kitchen. "I told you they'd be back," sang Poppy cheerily as they put us down gently onto the kitchen floor.

"Well, and where have you two been, I wonder," said Mum, placing a delicious looking saucer of milk down beside us. We slurped it up greedily. It certainly felt good to be back with the family again.

"My golden acorn!" I suddenly remembered it was at the bottom of my backpack outside under the flowerpot, I had to hide it somewhere safe. I scampered out of the cat flap with Polly on my heels.

"Off again," I heard Mum chuckle. "See you next week."

"Where are you going in such a hurry?" panted Polly.

"Oh—er, I thought that we should hide the—er backpacks before Mum and Dad find them," I replied awkwardly. "Tell you what; you go over to the barn ask Rob or Roy to run down to the pond and tell the others that we're having a meeting in the barn in about half an hour, Rob and Roy are to bring their storyboards, we've got to start writing our adventure whilst it still fresh in our memories."

"Wow! Now that we're finally home, that was some adventure we had, wasn't it?"

"Certainly was, but it's beginning to feel like it never happened, when's the next one?" replied Polly cheekily.

"Let's finish this one first, you go get the others, I'll hide these packs in the office and I'll meet you at the barn in about twenty minutes.

Polly disappeared through the hole in the fence, picking up the bags I walked slowly down to the shed at the bottom of the garden.

As I pushed the door open, I felt that someone else was there, sure enough Holly and Poppy were sitting on the two high-stools by the workbench waiting for me.

"You didn't take long," said Holly, "Where's Polly? I don't know, one saucer of milk and it's back to work for you two, don't you ever stop?"

"Anyway, we just can't wait to hear your story, can you type some of your adventure out for us right now?"

I dropped the bags and pushed them under the bench to be dealt with later, jumped onto the bench, and pulling open the cardboard wall to the office and quickly typed, "No, you'll have to wait."

"Oh, you spoil sport," said Poppy with a laugh, "Hey!' what do you think of this?" and she took away a second cardboard wall. There sat a second type writing machine.

"We saw it at a car-boot sale and just couldn't resist buying it for you, we know that you taught Lindy to type and now you can do your book twice as fast, oh and we got lots more paper with it too."

I tried out the new machine, typing out "Thanks a lot, you two are really great, wait until you read our adventure. We'll start writing it later when Lindy gets here."

At that moment we heard Mum's voice from the kitchen window, "Holly, Poppy, tea's ready!"

"Coming Mum," replied the girls, and turning to me Holly said, "See you in about half an hour, glad you like the new typewriter." And they both shot out of the door.

As soon as they were gone, I pulled my bag out from under the bench. Down at the bottom I found the little box that Bill Badger had given to me. It seemed so long ago now, and as Polly had said, almost like a dream.

I lifted the box out and studied it closely, it was made of a dark wood and had a small acorn carved neatly into the lid. I gently eased the lid open, with a quiver of excitement, and there, upon a cushion of thick dark green moss, lay the beautiful miniature golden acorn, all our adventures came flooding back to me in a moment.

I must have sat there gazing at it for quite a long time, as if in a magic spell. Finally, the spell was broken by the sound of Polly's voice shouting from the other side of the garden fence. "Come on, we're all waiting to start."

I quickly sprang up to the top shelf and hid the small box in the corner behind some old rubbish covered with cobwebs, and then went to join the others in the barn.

A fine autumn drizzle had set in, and I found the Barn Patrol settled comfortably in a circle of straw bales just inside the barn doors.

Rob and Roy had laid out their storyboards in two neat lines in the middle and were proudly explaining their pictures to the others.

"Crikey," I said, as I joined them, "Seeing all the pictures laid out together shows us just how much work you two have done. I'm going ask the girls to get Mum to make a carrot cake and you two can scoff the whole lot." The rats grinned at the thought.

"When you look at the sketches, it all comes flooding back," said Lindy, slowly moving from one picture to the next.

I stopped at one picture and looked a little more closely at it. It was a sketch of Bill Badger and myself standing at the edge of a forest clearing. It looked very much as if Bill Badger was secretly giving me something. "Oh, oh," I thought, as all the others gathered around me.

"This is the only picture that we can't figure out," said Polly. "Nobody noticed at the time, but Roy's caught you and Bill Badger looking rather suspicious, I'd say by the look of it that Bill's giving you a small object and he definitely doesn't want anybody to see what he's doing. Come on, Anna, what's the secret?"

Chapter 15
The Golden Acorn and the Book

I realised that my secret had been discovered. I knew all along that I was going to have to tell someone, so I decided to tell them all.

"Wait a minute," I said to them, and I hurried back to the shed to fetch the little wooden box.

When I returned, I found them all talking excitedly about Rob and Roy's wonderful sketches, they certainly did bring back to reality, all our strange adventures.

I coughed rather loud, "Right," I began. "Everybody sit down."

When they were all seated comfortably in a circle, I walked into the centre, and taking the small box from my bag, I opened it and walked round the circle showing it to each of them one at a time.

"This is what Bill Badger gave to me." I then proceeded to tell them the incredible story about Bill Badger, Midas Mole and the escape from the underground world of the Dooms with the two Golden Acorns and also of the planting of one of the acorns by Bill and the mole along the streams' course south of the dam.

"So that explains that wonderful Willow tree," said Roy.

"Is that why the crows followed us?" asked Lindy.

"No, I'm sure that they were just escorting us to the borders of their land, carrying out the orders from Baron Ubitz," I replied. "But I'm sure that if they had known we had this with us, then things would have gotten a little more serious."

"So, what are you going to do with it? Shall we plant it over by the spinney?" asked Polly, excited at the thought of having her very own Magic Willow Tree.

"No," I said. "Bill Badger and Morris mole have taken many risks to get the little acorn this far, it's up to us to try and finish the job for them."

"I'll hide it in the shed. We'll have to tell Poppy and Holly, they'll read it in the story anyway. We must all keep it secret."

"We mustn't say a word to anyone. None of us actually saw this Baron Ubitz, but I'm quite prepared to believe that he's somewhere down there under Wood-on-the-Hill, and just imagine if he found out about our secret, he'd probably send his bully boys over to invade the spinney and what would Mum and Dad have to say about that?"

Everybody looked at each other in serious disbelief.

"Well, I think that the sooner we pass this little treasure on, the better. But we shouldn't rush into anything in a hurry."

"Now, Polly, Lindy and I are going back to the shed to start typing, if I could take your storyboards rats that would be great. In the meantime, if you four rats are going down to the spinney this evening, I'm pretty sure that the storks will be dropping in; don't say anything to them about the acorn yet, leave that to me.

"You can tell them that we'll be having a splendid home coming party down there at midday tomorrow."

The three of us arrived back at the garden shed just as the two girls were coming out of the kitchen door. By the time they reached the shed, I had a note typed ready for them. It read:

Hi Poppy, Hi Holly,

Lindy says thank you for the new typewriter, we have had an exciting and sometimes terrifying adventure, but we all agree it was well worth it. If you look through the storyboards that Rob and Roy sketched on the way, it will give you some idea, the rest, you'll have to read as we write it.

I gave Holly the note and they sat down and began looking through the sketches, looks of surprise and wonder soon covered their faces.

When they had finished, they both turned to face us. I had another note ready for them before they could open their mouths:

The answer is, 'Yes it's true every picture you see tells a day-to-day story of our adventures.'

"What! The giant fish, the water rats, the crows, Badger and his friends…" started Poppy.

'Yes, all true,' I typed out hurriedly. 'You'll have to wait for the whole story to understand it all properly, pass us the sketches in order, you can see Rob and Roy have numbered them.'

So, Lindy and I tapped away into the evening, waking up early the following day to finish the first rough before 12 AM. Of course, we would have to rewrite it after everyone had read through it and added things that the three of us had missed out, but it was enough for the two girls who had been reading it with wonder as each line flipped out of the top of the typewriters.

They really could not quite believe it, not until I finally showed them the little carved box and the golden acorn.

'Look,' I typed, 'we're having a meeting cum party down at the spinney today, in fact, we're nearly late already. You must keep all this deadly secret, but do you think that Mum and Dad would let you come down to the spinney.'

"Oh yes," said Poppy. "We've been down there a few times since you've been away. Dad came with us the first time looking for you two, and Mum says it's okay as long as we don't go anywhere near the water."

So off we all scampered to meet the others down at the spinney.

They were all there waiting for us. Sam and Sidney were having a snack at the far end, Walt and Will were very much at home already and when we arrived, they all gathered around.

"This is a truly amazing adventure that you all have experienced," said Holly, holding out the typed copy, "and we both find it really hard to believe, but nobody could have made up such a story, and, of course, there is the Golden Acorn to prove that it is all true."

At the mention of the Golden Acorn, the others all looked at me with alarm.

"Don't worry, everybody," I said. "Holly and Poppy have to know, or we can't carry out the rest of Bill Badger's plan."

120

"And what might that be?" coughed Sam Stork as he swallowed the rest of his snack.

"Oh, sorry Sam," I said, and I quickly told Sam and Sidney the secret about the Golden Acorn and Bill Badger's plan for it to be sown as an experiment in a foreign country to finally prove its magical power.

"And what's more," carried on Poppy, "Mum and Dad have decided to take us on holiday to a place called Barbados, next March. It's very foreign and a long way away, so we can take the magic acorn and try out the second experiment.

Everyone seemed pretty pleased and somewhat relieved at this news, we all had our own ideas of what Baron Ubitz looked like and none of them were very pleasant, I think that we were all of the opinion that the sooner we could pass the Golden Acorn on the better. Not that we were cowards you understand, just a genuine fear of the unknown.

After that everybody relaxed and chatted eagerly amongst themselves. The girls fired question after question at the animals, Rob and Roy doing their best to answer by scratching quick sketches in the sand at the water's edge. Finally, Holly turned to me and said that she and Poppy would go back to the house and see what food and drink they could find to bring back to the party. I found a couple of matches in the bottom of Roy's backpack, and we got a little fire going, somebody found our old saucepan from somewhere and pretty soon we had one of our Barn Patrol mushroom, berry and nut soups on the boil, we found everything we needed not far away in the field and hedgerows.

Soon the girls arrived back with some more goodies and the party took off.

When everyone had eaten enough, we put some bigger logs on the fire and we all sat round quietly gazing into the embers as dusk slowly enveloped our little spinney.

Nobody noticed Poppy as she got to her feet, but when she gave a couple of coughs, she soon got everybody's attention, "Whilst you were away," she began, Holly and I have done some writing of our own. It's a little song about your adventure and the way we imagined it might be. It's nothing like what really happened. I'm afraid that you're not in it either," she said turning to Walt and Will, "Because we didn't know you then, anyway. Here goes…"

Holly got up and stood next to her little sister, and in the warm glow of the fire they sang this lovely song. They named it 'The Barn Patrol Blues' and Poppy had brought her guitar with her for accompaniment.

The Barn Patrol Blues

Two cats, two rats and a lamb
Decided to go for a ramble,
Over the fields and through the trees
Across the stream, right up to their knees,
Doing and playing exactly what pleased,
Two cats, two rats and a lamb.

Two cats, a lamb and two rats
Trekked off with their bulging packs,
Our adventurous chums were off to roam,

They returned to the stream, as dry as a bone,
They all sat down and thought of home,
Two cats, two rats and a lamb.

And when the sun went down,
A fire they slumbered around,
All cosy and tight, they slept through the night,
The sun brought the dawn, a stretch and a yawn,
A breakfast snack, back on with their packs,
Two cats, a lamb and two rats.

Now which way should they ramble?
Two cats, two rats and a lamb, all
Did agree, for they could see
The fields seemed strange, the bushes, the trees,
And all would die for a sip of tea,
Two cats, two rats and a lamb.

So they turned and headed for home,
The cats, the rats and the lamb,
And as they walked, they began to talk
Of homely things, of hop-scotch and chalk,
Their cosy pond, the old grey stork,
Tired cats, tired rats, tired lamb.

When they had finished, we all clapped furiously and cheered them for a long time. The two girls looked so pleased, after all, it was a great song, if not quite accurate, and Poppy was so cool on the guitar. It was an excellent way to round off the evening, we all said goodnight to Sam, Sidney, Walt and Will and strolled slowly back across the field, Sam and Sidney flopped in big cheerio circles above us and disappeared over the roof of the barn. We all went to bed; definitely home at last.

Life went back to normal after that, or sort of back to normal. Autumn progressed towards winter, all the leaves fell off the trees and everyone began to keep more into their cosy homes.

Although we all had our separate lives we were held together by our secret bond and the memories of our adventure. We found it difficult to lead normal lives with thoughts of Golden Acorns and Baron Ubitz buzzing around our heads, and we only felt relaxed when we were all together. So we did see quite a lot of each other. Sam told us that the foxes in the next field had left shortly after we departed on our adventure.

"Maybe they were summoned by Baron Ubitz," said Polly.

"Maybe they were," replied Sam. "But at least there's no…one to spy on you anymore and tell your secrets to those we don't want to know."

The story was re-typed and then typed again.

Holly said that it was so good that she'd like to show it to the mother of a friend of hers at school, this lady had a job in a book company and Holly thought our story so good that it might get printed for real.

'What about our secret?' I typed out.

Oh, we'll leave those bits out, there'll be enough for her to decide whether it's good enough. I'll have to ask the others, I thought.

So, I asked the others and they were all undecided, until Sam said that no harm could come of it as long as the important bits were left out. Everyone agreed to the idea after that. "Anyway," went on Sam, "wouldn't it be grand if the Barn Patrol managed to get their story printed; the first of many, eh? What do you think Anna, Polly and Lindy—Famous authors!" he said, chuckling away to himself.

And so it happened that Holly did take our story to school, and the lady did like it, and said that when we had finished it, she would show the story to her boss.

Then winter arrived with its icy fingers and sleety winds. The rats went off to sleep through it, Sam and Sidney flew south to warmer climates, they said. Log fires were lit in the house every day and we only went out for real once a week, and that was to see Lindy. She lived in a barn for the winter, over by the spinney. It was at one of these meetings that we decided that our book would not be finished until the family had returned from their holiday with the results of the second Acorn experiment.

Christmas came and went with all its fun. The snows fell, there was sledging with Holly and Poppy, snowmen and snowballing. Every day, I went and checked the little box on the top shelf. I even kept my hand in on the typewriter. I tried some poetry but nothing much good.

By the end of February, the girls were getting very excited about their holiday which was planned for the Easter holidays.

The date soon arrived; June, next door had been asked to look after us kittens. June's nice, she gives us different food from mum, and she spends the whole time fussing over us. Sam the spaniel went to the kennels, he loves it there, lots of mates he says, and the food and walks are great.

Everything was set, and as Holly picked me up to say goodbye, I slipped the little box into her hand. The taxi drove off and that was that.

About ten days later, there laying on the doormat with the rest of the post was a little letter with a Barbados stamp on it, it was addressed to:

Polly, Anna &The Barn Patrol

We picked it up and rushed down to the shed. When we opened it, we discovered, to our delight, a photograph of a beautiful palm tree standing proudly and slightly higher amongst a group of others on a lovely sandy beach, Holly and Poppy stood at the base of its trunk with big smiles on their faces, and looking very tanned.

There was a letter with it saying that they had planted the Golden Acorn the night they had arrived, and sure enough, the following morning, on the very spot they had planted the acorn, there was this wonderful tree. The girls called it the golden palm, but the local children had named it the Voodoo Palm; this was because they knew each tree by heart, and they immediately realised that there was something strangely magical about the arrival of this beautiful palm. Their parents were also in wonder, and I think the name voodoo may have come from them.

'The milk from its coconuts,' Holly wrote, 'tasted twice as sweet as that from the other trees and the sound of the sea breeze as it sung through its palm fronds played a sweeter note.'

The letter went on, saying that the family always sat under the golden palm, after a swim, it was their favourite spot and made them all feel so happy. Dad says he had never felt better and could easily stay there in the shadows for the rest of his life. The letter finished saying that they would bring us home a coconut, if they were allowed to bring it through the customs.

We showed the letter and photograph to Lindy and ten days later, we were all sitting in the shed waiting eagerly for the family's return. Sure enough, the girls rushed straight down to see us as soon as they arrived.

We all got a big hug and a beach hat, "Woven by one of the boys on the beach using leaves from the Golden Palm," said Poppy. "And we've got one each for all the others, I hope the sizes are right, although Sam and Sidney were hard to guess at. Oh, and they wouldn't let us through with the coconut."

We tried the hats on, and they fitted perfectly, Lindy closed her eyes, "It feels exactly the same as when we were under the Big Willow tree," she whispered, and we all agreed.

'Thanks for the hats,' I typed, 'and the letter, and the photo, and the experiment. We're all so pleased we can now finish the book and Sam can take a letter and a copy of the photograph to Bill Badger. I wonder what he will say?'

We finished our book and Holly's friend's mum thought that it was so good that she decided to publish it and even wanted to use Rob and Roy's pictures. She said that Holly and Poppy had amazing imaginations to be able to write such a wonderful adventure story. You see, we didn't want to tell the whole truth, and I didn't want to be famous, we just wanted to be happy, and we certainly were that.

Spring finally came again to the garden, and there was I dozing under the blue bush in the morning sun when a shadow suddenly blocked out the sun. I opened my eyes to see Sam and Sidney circling overhead. I took off my new hat and waved at them, as they disappeared over towards the spinney.

Great, I thought, the day we've been waiting for. I rushed into the shed, picked up a small package which we had prepared and shouted for Polly. She popped out from behind her favourite flowerpot. "What's up?" she said. "Have you come up with another adventure?"

"No," I replied, "Sam and Sidney are back and they've just headed over towards the spinney.

"Right, you get Rob and Roy, I'll go find Lindy," she said excitedly, and disappeared through the hole in the fence.

So the old Barn Patrol made its way, once more, across the backfield with hats on and staves in hand, Polly chasing the early spring butterflies as we went.

Sam, Sidney, Walt and Will were chatting together when we arrived, and we all sat down on the bank next to them. I produced the photograph and Sam said, "Well, that confirms all of Bill Badger's hopes, I wonder what he'll say when he sees this?"

"We were all thinking that ourselves," I said, "So I've prepared a parcel for him and we were wondering if you would mind flying it up to him, it's not very heavy."

"Of course we don't mind, and if we leave soon we should be there and back before dark."

Dark arrived at half past five and still no sign of the storks, so we all had a bit of a restless night worrying what had happened to Sam and Sidney. No need to really because they woke me from my morning snooze in the garden the following morning in exactly the same way at exactly the same time, I immediately grabbed the others and we all rushed down to the spinney.

Sam and Sidney were there.

"Bill Badger says thank you very much for carrying out the second experiment. He's so pleased that it was a success, but he's a bit puzzled as to what to do next.

"We caught him just as he was waking up from his winter sleep and he looked a little bit bleary eyed, but what he did say is that he hoped that he might see you all soon."

On hearing this, all the others turned towards me with excited looks on their faces.

"Oh no!" I said and closed my eyes in the lovely spring sunshine and dozed off.

Some weeks later, we were relaxing in the house after the evening meal when dad suddenly said, "Holly, I read that book that you and Poppy wrote. What imaginations you both have. You know, it's just the sort of thing that I imagine those two kittens of ours would get up to."

Poppy looked at me and Holly looked at Polly and we all looked at each other with a big wink and a secret smile.

THE END